DEAR SYLVIA, LOVE JANE

DETECTIVE MOLLY MALONE

ERIN HALL

For Amanda

CHAPTER
ONE

It was nearing seven in the evening that day in August 1943 when Molly Malone closed Bert Underwood's file. Even though it was a Friday the thirteenth Molly decided a closed case could only be a good omen.

After Bert had left the detective agency, Molly locked the door behind him. She pulled out her case files and updated her notes to detail how the meeting had gone.

Bert Underwood had long suspected his wife of stepping out on him. And boy was she. Most days when Bert left for work, the missus would entertain a visitor or two for a few hours before sending them on their way, as Molly discovered when she trailed Mrs. Underwood.

Sometimes Molly would follow Bert's wife to where she'd meet someone at a hotel. Usually her suitors were men, but she entertained women on occasion as well. Molly had even recognized one of Mrs. Underwood's female dalliances from her favorite underground gay club, a place called Whiskers.

Once Molly had collected reams of photos and documentation on the wife's adventures, she called Mr. Underwood back into the office.

Prior to Bert's arrival at the detective agency, Molly instructed James Hayward—her friend and colleague—on breaking the news to Bert gently.

"He'll be here any moment," Molly said to James as she prepared the front room of the agency office.

James emerged from the back office with a heavy sigh. He leaned against the doorframe. "You know how much I hate this part."

"You'll do brilliantly as always!" Molly bustled around the front room as she spoke, straightening papers and chairs. "Just...please *try* not to get him so distraught that he leaves without paying his bill." She closed a couple of file cabinet drawers that she'd rifled through earlier. The metal wheels squeaked softly along their tracks.

"It's like the client we had a few months ago," she went on. She unlocked the door that opened to the small hallway of the professional building they operated out of. "You remember, the lady who had trouble with her grown son," Molly reminded James. "You got her so worked up that she left in tears, and I had to hound her for weeks to get the rest of our payment."

"I remember," James said, and he tightened his necktie with precise fingers. "*She* was lovely. The son on the other hand was a *son of a*...well he was no good, that's for sure.

Remember he tracked us down after it was all over? Came in hollering at me—"

"It wasn't personal." Molly brushed aside James's frustration. "He was amped up on a little borrowed brass. Just *drunk* is all. Anyway, we handled it, didn't we? And finally got paid!" Molly, a foot shorter than James, looked up at her friend's face and smoothed his salt-and-pepper beard with a smile. "I promise you'll be fine. Just keep an eye on the signals. I'll tell you if you're off track."

———

By the time the client arrived, Molly was seated behind a secretary's desk in the front room. "Good afternoon, Mr. Underwood. I'll tell him you're here."

"Afternoon," Bert mumbled, nervously shifting his hat in his hands. He sat stiffly in one of the wooden chairs along the wall, facing the desk where Molly was seated. With her softly curled hair and prim sweater and scarf, she looked every bit the part of a detective's secretary.

Molly cracked open the door to the back room of the agency where James sat waiting. "He's here, Mr. Hayward."

Once Bert disappeared to the back room, Molly opened the top drawer of the secretary's desk and flipped a switch on a small metal box that fit neatly in the depths of the drawer. The two men's voices emitted from a tiny speaker attached to the box. She adjusted the volume down slightly. The whole contraption was no bigger than a pack of cards.

James's voice came through the speaker softly. "Mr. Underwood, your assumptions were correct. She's been two-timing you."

There was silence, then the shuffling of some papers. Molly could imagine Bert flipping through her photographs with the posture of a broken man. She kicked her feet up on the wooden desk and adjusted the back seam of her nylons as she listened.

"With the mailman, even?" Bert cried. Even through the tinny speakers in Molly's desk drawer, she heard the anguish in his voice. "And who's *this* guy?" His voice rang at an even higher register.

Molly reached into the drawer and flipped one of two toggle switches near the speaker. The wires from the switch box reached to the back of the drawer, where they emerged from a small drilled hole to snake down the desk's leg. The wires then ran under the thin rugs of the waiting room floor before emerging briefly to climb the wall, snug to the doorframe leading to the back office where James and Bert Underwood now sat.

Now that she'd toggled the switch, Molly knew a small red light would be shining above the doorframe in the back room, out of the client's sight, but where James could clearly see it from his desk. That red light meant James was supposed to redirect the conversation.

"You really saw her do all this?" Bert Underwood was weary.

"With my own two eyes, Underwood," James said without skipping a beat. "But look here," he continued. "When you first came in to see me, you were hoping for evidence to make that divorce you wanted turn out in your favor. Do you remember that?"

"You're right."

Molly flipped the toggle for the red light back to its neutral position, then briefly toggled the other switch on and off. This switched triggered the green light. *Nice work, James.*

Through the speaker she heard James continue. "With what you have here, you won't have to pay her a cent. I know it hurts now, but you're saving yourself more heartache in the long run."

After a few more exchanges, Molly heard the scraping of chairs as the men rose from their seats. James and Bert would be coming out of the room shortly. She quickly switched off the speaker and quietly closed the top drawer of the desk, then turned to a stack of files in front of her.

As the door to the back room opened, James said, "After it's all done you should take yourself for a nice holiday. Somewhere with palm trees."

Bert brightened slightly. "Palm trees?"

"And drinks with umbrellas in them," James said. "After all, this should be a time of celebration for you, should it not? Miss Malone, be a dear and close out Mr. Underwood's file, would you?" He turned to shake Bert's hand. "Good day, sir. And good luck." James disappeared back into the back office and closed the door.

Left alone in the front room with Bert, Molly pushed a slip of paper across the desk toward him. "Here's your balance due, Mr. Underwood. Would you like a receipt?"

Bert looked blankly at the paper, his mind perhaps still

on palm trees and drinks with umbrellas. "That's not necessary, thank you."

Now, as Molly finished her notes on the Underwood case, she murmured as she wrote. "Client paid in full and left satisfied…with the results…of the investigation." She filed the papers in the drawer marked U-V-W, then closed the drawer with a satisfying click.

That done, Molly sauntered to the back room where James was leaning over the desk with a newspaper in front of him. "Friday the thirteenth or not, how about a drink?"

"Way ahead of you, boss." He held up a short, crystal-cut highball glass that sloshed an amber liquid.

"Cheers, then! Pour me one too. I couldn't have done it without you, pal!"

James pulled the bottle from the bottom drawer along with a glass that matched his own and poured a few glugs for Molly.

"I don't understand why you don't get a *normal* job." He handed Molly the highball glass that looked tiny in his hands, large in hers. "Like in a shop. Or even back at the station."

"You know perfectly well why I can't get a job in a shop. I'd die of boredom," Molly said as she clinked her glass against James's. "And the station is no better. They'd stick me behind a desk again, answering phones and typing reports. I'm much better at *pretending* to be a secretary than actually being one."

James smiled at his friend. "Even as a *pretend* secretary, you're not very good."

"At the very least, I *look* the part. That should count for something!" Outside the office windows, the streetlights kicked on, illuminating the room with a soft yellow glow. "Let's hit Whiskers," Molly said. "I'll buy you something better than this swill."

"Can't." James quickly gulped down his drink. "Lewis is waiting for me at home. He's making something special for dinner." James stood and pulled his suit jacket from the back of the chair.

"I'll see you tomorrow night then?" Molly asked.

James frowned. "Tomorrow? That's my and Lewis's anniversary. I've told you." He shrugged his jacket on and made his way to the front room of the agency.

"Only for an hour then," Molly powered on. She took a gulp of whiskey, following closely behind James as he attempted an exit. "It's the policeman's banquet and they'll all be congratulating each other, clapping each other on the back...all that nonsense. I need you to get friendly with the officers we haven't worked with. We need more cases. And I can't drum up business on my own."

"Molly, I *can't*." There was an edge to his voice. James draped his overcoat over his arm and took his hat from the wooden rack near the door.

Molly gathered her own coat and purse, ignoring James's frown. She quickly finished shutting down the office for the weekend. "I promise to make it up to you. I'll buy you and Lewis the finest bottle of champagne I can find!"

James made no response but shuffled his hat in his hands.

Finally, Molly broke the silence. "Look, I know you don't *love* this work. But after a few more cases I'll be ready to come clean…to tell the *truth* about the business. That it's actually *me* working these cases. In any case, my paperwork *is* legal, even if yours isn't. But first I have to get my footing. Then you'll be off the hook for good, I promise. With enough closed cases on the books, I'll show the guys at the station that I really *can* do this. But without their referrals and cooperation, detectives dry up. And I can't—"

"Fine."

Molly brightened. "Oh, James, you're absolutely the best. If we both weren't gay, I'd propose."

James snorted. "I wouldn't accept."

James and Molly parted ways for the night. After locking the detective agency door behind her, Molly emerged onto Ohlone Street, just a few blocks from North Beach where Whiskers was tucked away off a side street.

Ohlone was a short street that spanned a few blocks of private business offices and scraping-to-get-by professionals, such as Molly and James. She let herself get enveloped into the casual bustle of evening pedestrians on the sidewalk.

As she walked in the growing darkness of the summer evening, Molly thought about Bert Underwood's wife. Not in a salacious way, but because she could relate to her.

Both Molly and the soon-to-be-ex-Mrs. Underwood understood the roles they were expected to play in life. They went along with them for a short time, but ultimately, they both rejected them. Only in Mrs. Underwood's case, she'd gotten caught. And Molly planned on *never* getting caught.

She had crafted her business perfectly. James was the front man, brought in to pose as the detective when a client expected to see a male face. He was paid handsomely for it. And when they first started the gig a year prior, James had enjoyed the opportunity to practice his acting skills.

But Molly knew it was beginning to wear on him. He didn't love the work like she did. After all, she got to do the fun part—trailing people, gathering intel, following her hunches to uncover hidden secrets. Meanwhile, James had to handle clients' emotions at the start and finish of each case. Not that Molly would mind doing that part too. Eventually.

But for now, she knew her clients needed to see a man behind the detective's desk or there would be no clients at all. No one would hire a female private investigator. But Molly didn't see what the fuss was about if clients simply *thought* the detective they were hiring was James Hayward instead of Molly Malone. As long as the work was sound, the clients were happy and payments were collected—there was no need for anyone to know the truth.

Now, making her way through the San Francisco night, Molly relished her lot in life: exciting work, good friends, and a bar not far from the office where she could sip a nice whiskey among folks like herself.

Though her feet ached from a long day of running around town in her stacked heel oxfords, Molly walked briskly toward Whiskers in the cooling August evening. Over the years, the club had become as familiar and comfortable to her as her own apartment. Going to Whiskers felt like going home.

And yet, there was a marked difference between the entryways of the two locations. While Molly's apartment building boasted a welcoming front gate with a lush garden courtyard, Whiskers remained hidden on purpose.

CHAPTER
TWO

In a dark alley underneath a creaking fire escape ladder, a short set of steps led down to the basement entrance of a gritty, nondescript building. To the typical passerby, this bland gray door in an alley wouldn't have made an impression. But if you were in the know, like Molly was, the world behind that door held a warmth, excitement, and sense of kinship the larger world knew nothing about.

Tucking herself next to the closed door that led to Whiskers, Molly rapped on the door.

Tap tap-tap.

The knock had changed a couple of weeks before, but she'd had plenty of time to use it since then, so she knew she'd done it right. The door cracked open, and Molly immediately smiled at Natalia Fazio's face, which broke into a grin when she saw Molly at the door.

"Hi honey!" Natalia ushered Molly in.

Molly hugged her. "You're security tonight, huh?"

"At your service, ma'am." Natalia bowed slightly. "You look dapper tonight. Meeting someone special?"

Molly laughed and shrugged off her moss-colored tweed overcoat. She draped it over her arm. "Just you and Paula, my nightly crew."

Natalia nodded at Molly's holstered gun, now revealed after she'd removed her jacket. "You know I don't like that heat you pack. It reminds people you're a cop."

Molly gave a good-natured grin. "I'm not a cop." She lightly squeezed the gun against her rib cage with her left elbow. She hadn't fired it in years.

"Close enough." Natalia shrugged, then smiled again. "Much as I'd love to see you find a nice girl to settle down with, I know it would mean seeing less of you around here. And we need regulars like you to keep the lights on."

"I'm happy to help, my friend." She gave Natalia's arm a light squeeze.

With the door closed behind her, Molly let her eyes adjust to the dim light and slowly took in the scene before her. The short candles on the tables glowed through red glass, casting flickering shadows among the patrons. It wasn't a busy night, not yet. But still, there were several people in the bar, sipping cocktails and leaning close to one another. The cool air in the dark space was a welcome relief against the city's summer heat. Music softly trickled from the jukebox.

Molly found a seat at the bar near the wall. From the other end of the bar, Natalia's cousin and the owner of Whiskers, Paula Fazio, held up a bottle of whiskey as a question. Molly nodded.

As usual, Paula was wearing a white button-down shirt and suspenders. Her tailored slacks fit her nicely, and men's brogues peeked out from below the cuffs of her pantlegs. Even though Paula had been thrown in jail at least twice for wearing clothes that didn't match the gender on her ID, she'd never let her self-expression be dampened. Besides which, her powerful underground connections made it difficult for the police to target her directly too often. Others, of course, weren't released as easily as Paula Fazio.

"Thanks," Molly said when Paula set her whiskey and rocks in front of her. "I've missed your heavy pours the last few nights. What have you been up to?"

"Fazio family business," Paula said with an easy smile. Molly knew that meant she shouldn't ask any more questions.

Molly sipped her drink, feeling the familiar fire light up her sternum.

"Meeting anyone special tonight?" Paula asked.

Molly squinted at her old friend. "Not you too! Natalia asked the same thing. Can't a girl dress dapper on occasion without being on the make?"

Paula laughed. "I suppose so. But I do wonder about you, Molly. In all the years I've known you, you've only entertained a couple broads. And casually at best. No one steady. What gives?"

Molly waved away Paula's question. "I get by just fine. Besides, I got work."

"Work isn't love, toots."

There was a heavy pause.

Molly and Paula didn't talk too much about work, given the near-to-conflicting nature of their lines of business. While Paula's family dealt in activities that varied in their degrees of legality, Molly Malone was closely connected to law enforcement. While not being a police officer herself, her profession as a private investigator was close enough to the law to keep Paula from discussing her family's affairs with Molly.

Over the years, Molly and Paula talked about the weather, how well the Giants were or were not playing, whiskey, women, the war. More recently, they pontificated about the Zoot Suit Riots in Los Angeles and the stunning new dance shows at the Forbidden City nightclub in Chinatown. They talked about Molly's hometown of Portland, Oregon. What they didn't talk about was work. Without saying so, they both understood that any talk of business would only complicate their friendship. As long as the whiskey flowed, the easiness between them remained.

There was a *tap tap-tap* at the front door.

Molly and Paula turned to watch as Natalia cracked the door open, said a few words to whoever it was, and then let in a tall, thin man in a checked sport coat. Molly didn't recognize him.

She turned back to her whiskey and took a sip, knowing the booze itself came from Paula's notorious "family business."

As a bar that catered to butches and femmes, gay cats and fairies, and queers of all stripes, the Whiskers crowd was always only one wrong turn away from trouble. As

Paula well knew, jail time was common for anyone wearing the "wrong clothes." Short of that, anyone suspected of same-sex activity or proclivities were liable to be harassed by police or beaten. Or worse.

Gathering together in one spot was risky because it only invited suspicion. But Paula's routine of changing the passcode knock at Whiskers helped a great deal. Every so often, she would establish a new knock code to grant entry. Word would spread among the regulars and there'd be a grace period of a few days while everyone got used to it. If someone came along without the right knock, it was Natalia's job to bar entrance. She would determine if it was someone who simply hadn't been to Whiskers for too long to know the code or if it was someone looking for trouble. And at nearly six feet tall, with a muscular build and a grand tumble of dark curls springing from under her cap, Natalia was not often taken for an easy target.

Now that Molly's eyes had fully adjusted to the low lamplights and candle flames, the bright colors of the bar and the patrons revealed themselves. She settled into a familiar, easy posture, leaning against the bar while she sipped the smooth whiskey. The nightlife in Whiskers was a soothing balm on the rash of the larger world outside. Like Molly, the other patrons seemed to become more themselves when inside the walls of the dark basement bar.

People would often enter dressed one way, immediately disappear into the back bathrooms, and return moments later dressed in their most fabulous expression of themselves. Suits were exchanged for slinky ballgowns, makeup was removed or applied, high heels were swapped for low work shoes, and vice versa. It wasn't unusual for male and female friends to exchange outfits on the spot, laughing all the while, relieved to be in a safe place at last among friends and chosen family.

For several slow rounds of cocktails, Molly stuck fast to the barstool, sipping whiskey until she felt all was right in the world again. Around her, soft, slow music floated from the jukebox. A few couples danced closely together. At tables and booths, groups or couples held low conversations with occasional bouts of riotous laughter. Some couples sat quietly holding one another, drinks forgotten in front of them.

Then a knock at the door froze all life in Whiskers.

Tap-tap tap tap-tap.

The knock was wrong. Very wrong.

Molly and the others instantly knew this. But it wasn't a tap from only a few weeks before, as sometimes happened when someone hadn't been in for a while. This was an *old* knock. It must have been. Or a complete guess. Either way, it sucked the joy from the room in an instant.

Molly watched Natalia and Paula lock eyes from across the bar. Then Natalia cracked the door open, filling the open frame with her body. Molly released the snap that wrapped around the butt of her gun, but she kept her weapon holstered. The action made her heart beat thickly, but she forced herself to breathe steadily.

Natalia spoke quietly at the door for several moments. Inside, patrons began to softly return to their conversations, sure that if it had been real trouble, it would have already erupted.

Finally, Natalia stepped aside to let in a man of average height and build.

The newcomer scanned the room, then smiled upon seeing the man in the checked sport coat and joined him at his table. But when Molly saw who it was, her heart quickened. She recognized him by his gait and sandy blond hair.

Detective Thomas Parker.

The last time she'd seen Thomas was at the police station over a year prior. They'd had a fine working relationship for a few years. Molly worked as Thomas's secretary and sometimes helped him with his undercover work. But one night Molly saw him with another man at Whiskers. Until then, Molly didn't know he was interested in men. But when Thomas saw Molly too, all the joy dropped from his face, and he quickly rushed out of the club. The next day at work, Molly discovered she'd been abruptly transferred to a different department. He refused to take her calls or make time for her when she stopped by his desk. If she passed him in the hallways, Thomas wouldn't speak to her or even look at her.

And until now, Molly hadn't seen him in Whiskers again.

Now, she watched Thomas as he briefly embraced the man in the checked sport coat before they settled into cozy conversation. Paula returned, standing across the bar from Molly. She began stacking an armful of clean tumblers on the bar in front of her. Together they watched Thomas and the other man conversing closely.

"Every day I see unfamiliar faces in here," Paula said. "I know I should be grateful. But it makes me nervous. You can never tell when bad business is underway until it's too late."

"Getting too popular for your own good?" Molly asked wryly.

Paula nodded. "It's quite a parlor trick. How to stay afloat with enough customers without drawing too big of a crowd. More people means more opportunity for the wrong kind to slip in."

"Anyone new you're worried about?"

"Not patrons so much as vice squad. I've heard they're getting rougher than usual these days. Of course, they'd never touch Whiskers, but sometimes there's a rogue cop who tries to get nosy. Nothing my family can't handle, of course. The cops and the Fazios…we have an understanding." Paula paused, though she clearly had more on her mind that she seemed to be debating sharing with Molly. She poured a short drink for herself and downed it.

"Between you and me?" she began, and Molly nodded. "There's something shady going on lately. More places are getting raided. Cops went in hard on Duke's—it's that cute joint in the Tenderloin. Run by a guy I've met once or twice. Anyway, they threw everyone in jail for the night, took all the booze from the shelves and the cash from the drawers. Made a mess of the place. But that's not the worst of it. Some others have gone missing."

"Others?" Molly asked.

"Bar owners. Feared dead, in fact. My buddy Walter owns the Hot Spot in the Mission. He called me the other day, spooked. He said he feared he was being followed. Asked if my family could do anything. 'Course they wouldn't—we don't get involved unless it's one of our own. I just told him to keep an eye out, maybe start carrying protection if it makes him feel better." Paula shrugged. "I feel bad for Walter, but I don't know what else I can do."

Molly kept her face neutral, listening to her friend. She'd never been to Duke's or the Hot Spot, but of course she'd heard of them. Hearing that there was a growing fear among proprietors of her community's gathering places worried her. But more than that, hearing Paula talk openly about what the Fazio family would and would not get involved with gave her a chill. She could guess at their arrangement with local law enforcement because it was the same everywhere. Underground operations of all kinds paid beat cops in order to remain in business, whatever their business might be: booze, sex, poker, opium—sometimes all that and more.

Though Molly felt close to Paula and Natalia, she couldn't imagine having a business relationship with the Fazios. From what Molly guessed, working with the Mafia was more dangerous than their protection was worth.

Paula shook her head to clear it, then saw Molly's empty glass. "Another one?"

"No," Molly said,. "Thanks, Paula. I need to get going. I'll see you next time."

On the way out, Molly made a point of walking slowly

near where Thomas Parker was seated. He glanced up at her as she passed, his eyes going wide for a moment when he registered the sight of her.

Molly paused at his table, unsure what to do or say to someone she'd been so close with once, someone she'd counted as a friend and colleague, who then had turned on her.

Though he looked straight at her, Thomas didn't acknowledge her. Instead, he turned back to the man he was with and shrugged his shoulders as though he'd never seen Molly before in his life.

CHAPTER
THREE

The next morning, Molly woke to discover she'd slept in her office. After finally ungluing herself from her barstool at Whiskers, Molly had begun a slow, meandering trek through the city toward her apartment. But as she passed by Ohlone Street, she decided a catnap on the cot in the office sounded more heavenly than trudging home several more blocks to her apartment.

She must have dozed harder than she meant to and slept there all night. As the sunlight screamed through the office windows, Molly put the cot away, ran a comb through her hair, and drank some water from the glass carafe on the bureau.

Then, slipping on her brown oxfords, Molly headed for the door. She reached for the handle, then paused.

The silhouette of a woman on the other side suddenly filled the door's frosted glass window. Molly stepped back and watched the woman hesitate before the door. When she finally knocked, it was Molly's turn to hesitate.

It was Saturday. The agency was closed. Perhaps she should keep quiet and wait for the woman to leave. She could let her come back on Monday when James would be here. After all, it was early, and she was still slightly sauced from the night before.

After a brief moment, Molly decided she could easily redirect a new client to coming back at a better time.

She unlocked and opened the door. The woman revealed on the other side of the door was dressed in a dramatic black-and-red dress with a wide-brimmed hat perched on her coiffed dark hair. It was altogether too much for an everyday look, certainly this early in the morning, but Molly soon learned this was how the lady always dressed.

"Oh, thank goodness," the woman said, her voice tinged with fear or relief—Molly couldn't tell which.

"Good morning," Molly said, letting the woman inside. "Are you alright? Have a seat."

The woman unpinned her hat and placed it delicately on the hat rack, tossing her curls softly and patting her head to smooth any flyaways. She sat in one of the sturdy wooden chairs across from Molly's desk.

Molly set a glass of water in front of the woman while she studied her potential client. This woman was poised but had a frantic energy about her. Her gaze fluttered around, taking in the room without seeming to land on anything. A sign of nervousness. She was clearly distraught.

"Thank you," the woman said, picking up the glass of

water with a gloved hand and taking a sip. "I feel simply awful about barging in so early…" She paused, and for a brief moment, Molly found herself in a locked gaze with the beautiful woman—flushed and slightly out of breath—who was now seated in front of her.

Molly permitted herself to let her eyes linger a moment longer. This was always a risk, of course—there were unspoken limitations to how long a woman like Molly could look directly into another woman's eyes. Gaze too long and they often became uncomfortable. But there's a microsecond that only queer people know about, when two people gaze at each other a shadow of a second longer than socially acceptable. But that moment had come and gone and Molly and whoever this woman was were still gazing softly at each other's faces, both mouths slightly agape.

The stranger broke away first, bringing an ivory-colored handkerchief to her bright nose and flushed cheeks. "I…I wasn't even sure you'd be open," she said. "But thank God you are."

"Actually, we're not," Molly said. "Not on the weekends. I just happened to be stopping by this morning. To tidy up."

"The detective isn't in?" She looked to be on the verge of tears again.

"Unfortunately, no. He won't be back in the office until Monday morning. But I can take down your name and phone number and he'll give you a call. I'm the detective's secretary. Name's Molly Malone." Molly stuck out her hand to shake with the woman, then realized she was being overly formal and regretted it, feeling silly.

The woman simply looked at Molly's outstretched hand in mild confusion. Then she dropped her poise and slumped in her chair. "Oh." She was silent for a moment.

"What's your name, ma'am?" Molly asked, taking out a notepad.

"Sylvia Owens," she said. "But he can't call me at home." Tears filled Sylvia's eyes anew. "Isn't there any way you can contact him now? I really do need to speak to him. It's about my husband, he—" She broke off, bit a gloved knuckle, and pulled the handkerchief to her mouth again.

At the mention of husband, Molly's heart swiftly clammed up. *Of course she'd have a husband.* Molly had never seen this woman at Whiskers, nor could she imagine her at any other gay bar in town. Molly must have misread the lingering gaze they'd shared. *Not that Mrs. Underwood had any trouble having fun, despite having a husband.* Still, there was something in Sylvia's presence that made Molly feel, much to her annoyance, like she wanted to help her, even if just to be near her.

"Mrs. Owens, I'm terribly sorry. The detective doesn't work on the weekends." Molly imagined that at this very moment, James would be in bed with Lewis, both of them just waking up. Together they'd be planning an elaborate dish to conjure up for their Saturday breakfast. After an evening of whiskey and mixed nuts from the bar, one of Lewis's homecooked meals sounded mighty fine.

"Would you like to tell me what you need?" Molly asked. "As the detective's secretary, I assist with paperwork, so I'd hear about it eventually. As I said, I'm Molly." She laid a hand softly over Mrs. Owens's trembling hand to bring her back into the moment. "What's troubling you, Mrs. Owens?"

"Sylvia, please," she said, looking at Molly once again. "I suppose there's no harm in telling you." She broke off her gaze and let her eyes flit about the room. "Let me just take a moment."

"Of course, Sylvia. Take all the time you need."

Molly had been in this situation before: a woman crying in front of her, Molly's heart disintegrating into powder until she could fix whatever was troubling her. But she had decided long ago that she was quite done with crying over women, or allowing women to cry over her, for that matter. Whoever this Mrs. Owens was, Molly intended to approach her on business terms.

Get it together, Malone. Molly turned her attention back to the notepad in front of her and the woman who was speaking. She tried to focus on the words Sylvia said, and not on the way her mouth moved as she spoke.

"Like I said, it's my husband," Sylvia began. "I'm terribly worried." She paused.

"Is he in trouble?" Molly asked.

Sylvia shook her head. "That's not what I mean. He's not in trouble. He's—I'm scared of him. He's been acting...strange..."

Molly set her notepad down and took a breath. "I'm getting a little confused, Sylvia. Let's slow down and take it from the top. What brought you in today, to seek out the services of a private detective?"

She was right to pause. Sylvia wasn't being straight with her, but it wasn't in the way she'd imagined. Typically, this was the time when clients would lay out their story in full force: all gory details and names and dates. But when asked directly, Sylvia had faltered, as though she was searching for her story. That alone was enough to efficiently scrub away the budding heart palpitations Molly had briefly felt. In no time at all, she began to see through Sylvia's act. The hair, the dress, the whole charade—she wanted someone to spy on her husband for reasons unknown. Yet she hadn't taken the time to come up with a plausible story.

Molly realized she was rejecting Sylvia's case before she even got started. But she felt justified—it *was* Saturday, and they *were* closed. As much as she and James needed more work, right now Molly wanted to finally get home, take a bath, and enjoy her weekend.

She tucked a loose strand of hair behind her ear. She wouldn't get distracted by women again, especially not married ones who gazed at her for too long. *Not again*, she vowed, sitting up straighter.

"He's trying to kill me," Sylvia said, locking eyes once more with Molly. Her tears had stopped, though her cheeks remained damp and slightly shiny.

There was something in Sylvia's look that gave Molly pause again. Perhaps she was telling the truth after all. *Maybe I'm losing my touch.*

She took notes as Sylvia told her story. "My husband

has hated me for years. But he won't divorce me. He likes having me around to torture," she said with a grimace. "I don't mean physically. It's always mind games and manipulation. Recently, it's escalated. There's been a man... following me, someone I've never seen before. At first, I thought nothing of it. Perhaps someone new in the neighborhood. But when Carl—that's my husband—when Carl was out the other day, this man came to my front door."

"What happened?" Molly asked. She took a sip of water. Her head was beginning to throb from the night before.

"I saw who it was through the window, and I was afraid to answer the door. But he came around the back through the kitchen. He attacked me!" Sylvia had been looking into the far distance as she spoke, clutching her handkerchief tight.

"How dreadful," Molly said, still slightly unsure of Sylvia's story. "Were you able to fight him off?"

Sylvia paused. "Somehow, yes. I...I don't know how, but he—he stopped and left."

"Did he say anything to you during this time?"

Sylvia's eyes darted, searching the corners of the office again. "He...he said, 'I'm going to kill you.'" She began sobbing again, softly, hiding her face in her gloved hands.

At this point, Molly didn't know what to believe. Her head wasn't in the right spot for all of this so early on a hungover Saturday morning. Maybe she was just tired. Maybe there *was* something to Sylvia's story after all. She did seem to be in a fair amount of distress and was going to great lengths for help, whatever was happening.

"Sylvia, I'm terribly sorry to hear this has happened to you," Molly said. "Now, please don't think me cruel with the questions I'm going to ask. These are standard questions that...*the detective* would ask you for clarification. So we might as well get started now."

Sylvia dabbed at her cheeks with the ivory handkerchief. "I understand."

"Alright." Molly flipped the page of her notepad. "If I'm understanding this right, you say you began to see this man around your neighborhood, and he seemed to turn up everywhere you went."

"That's right."

"Then one day he shows up at your house and helps himself to your hospitality. He says he's going to kill you and tries to do so. But you fight him off and he leaves."

Sylvia nodded.

"Let me ask you this, then. Why do you think your *husband* is behind this?"

Sylvia's posture changed. She straightened her back to sit upright and looked at Molly. "Oh. Well...when the man said he was going to kill me...he *also* said that Carl told him to do it. That *Carl* told him when he'd be gone and when he should come to do it." Her voice rose an anxious octave.

"I see." Molly put her notepad and pencil down. *No, definitely not losing my touch. This woman is a con artist, and not a very good one. She may be nice to look at, but she's angling for something, and I don't care to find out what.*

She watched Sylvia for a moment more, while the

damsel attempted to compose herself. "Well, Mrs. Owens—"

"Sylvia."

"*Sylvia.* I will pass along your information and your story to the detective on Monday. But I can't guarantee he'll take your case. If you'd rather he not call you at home, you are welcome to call Monday morning to talk to him." Molly stood and retrieved Sylvia's hat from the rack by the door.

Sylvia stood quickly and faced Molly, stepping close to her. "Oh please! You must tell him to help me. It's the only way." She grasped Molly's hands, her hat still dangling from Molly's grip.

The touch of Sylvia's grasp was electric. Molly didn't dare let down her guard.

"If someone attacked you, especially in your own house, why not call the police?" Molly released Sylvia's hands from her own and handed her the big black hat. "Why hire a private detective? If your husband is out to get you like you said, it would all come out in the investigation of the attack."

"I can't go to the police." Sylvia's voice changed. She spoke plainly now, the emotion in her voice transformed from frantic to bitter. "He's friends with them all. He pays them off in exchange for political favors. He's snaking his way up the political chain because he's too stupid to do it the upstanding way. So he throws his money around instead." Her eyes searched Molly's. "Isn't there some way you can convince the detective to take my case? *Please.*"

Molly opened the door. "You can call on Monday, Sylvia. Any time after nine in the morning."

She closed the door behind Sylvia, though trace scents of cigarette smoke and face powder lingered. Despite her best efforts, Molly felt a butterfly or two in her belly and a slight weakness in her knees.

CHAPTER
FOUR

The banquet hall vibrated with conversation, music, and the clinking of glasses and silverware against china. Clouds of cigarette smoke formed over clusters of people who spoke in joyful tones. The hall was filled with police officers, city council members, local dignitaries, and their wives.

"You've just missed my husband," Molly Malone said, indicating the man's suit coat she had draped over her arm. "He's new. In Homicide. He was *supposed* to be refreshing my drink." Molly emitted a practiced bubbly laugh. Around her, men and women in fancy attire mingled about the banquet hall. "I'm sure he'll be back any moment. Go on, Herbert, you must tell me more about what you do in Forensics. It's terribly fascinating!"

The man in the tan tweed suit pushed his glasses up on his nose and scratched his balding scalp. "Well, like I said, I review captures of fingerprints that our officers have taken in the field and compare those to our files of known criminals in hopes of securing a match."

"You must have eagle eyes for that job!" Molly said.

The man peered at Molly through the thick lenses of his glasses. "Ah, well. My vision is much better up close." He looked at his empty champagne flute. "If you'll excuse me, ma'am. It was lovely chatting with you."

"Certainly." Molly watched him shuffle off and made a mental note to write a letter on James's behalf to Herbert in Forensics to make a professional connection.

A few yards away, James lingered near the hors d'oeuvres. He held a tiny plate in one large hand while the other delicately picked up a dip-laden cracker. His naturally flushed face shone above his bright white shirt-collar. Near James, a white-haired man in a blue suit was piling food onto a plate.

Shoveling the cracker in his mouth, James's gaze locked onto Molly's. Molly subtly nodded her head toward the white-haired man.

With a mouthful of cracker and dip, James rolled his eyes and sighed, then turned to the man and introduced himself. At six feet, three inches tall, with a beefy build, James was used to towering over most others around him. The white-haired man gaped up at James's red face and shook his hand.

Satisfied that James would at least attempt to make a professional connection, Molly turned her attention back to the rest of the banquet hall.

There were at least a dozen tables set with crisp white linen, fine china and crystal, and enormous flower arrangements in the center of each. The women in the room, dressed in mink stoles, gloves, pearls, and hats of all shapes and sizes, were wives of police officers and other city government officials.

All except Molly, of course.

There was no plausible reason that a private investigator's *secretary* should be at such an event. So Molly invented a husband on the force who always seemed to be just out of sight. And given her previous employment in the police department, showing up without a disguise was out of the question.

Her heart pounded with each new interaction. Before leaving her apartment, Molly had donned the most house-wife-out-on-the-town dress she had—a navy blue woolen gown that draped elegantly from her shoulder to her waist, which was encircled by a thin leather belt. The dress hit just below her knees. The damn thing itched to high heaven and was much too warm for the summer evening. Molly was already eager to change back to her typical attire of linen slacks paired with a light sweater. But for now, she'd endure. Her officer's wife look was completed with white-rimmed glasses, jewelry she kept around for just such an occasion, and a nondescript but realistic wig of straight brown hair. She looked perfectly forgettable.

In the banquet hall, she recognized some faces from her time as Thomas's secretary in Criminal Investigations. She steered clear of anyone familiar in case they recognized her. The last thing she needed was someone blowing her cover.

The murmur of the crowd buzzed around Molly's head. Her cheeks were warm from the champagne.

She was considering who to approach next when she saw Thomas Parker. He was looking directly at her, and in an instant, Molly knew she'd been made.

Of course, she thought. *I wore this wig on the last case I helped him with before he sacked me.* Molly's legs went cold as she stared back at Thomas, his sandy blond hair combed neatly to match his put-together look. Not terribly different than how he looked the night before at Whiskers.

Thomas was seated at a table with his wife, herself in a housewife-out-on-the-town dress, and several other couples who were talking amiably with each other.

But Thomas looked directly at Molly with no indication of what he might be thinking.

At that moment, the recorded music faded out and someone at the front of the room spoke into a microphone. "Ladies and gentlemen, please begin finding your seats. We'll begin with tonight's speaker shortly."

The crowd bubbled with renewed excitement. Thomas returned his attention to his table. Molly turned to find James again, but he was already standing beside her.

"Oh!" she cried in alarm.

"You okay, boss?" James asked quietly. "You suddenly look more like hell than usual."

"I'll tell you later. Let's find seats." Molly shook off the distraction of Thomas. "We can't sit together though. You know how *my husband* is. That temper!"

Molly and James sat at adjacent tables but with their chairs turned toward the elevated stage at the front of the hall, so they effectively sat next to each other while appearing to be perfect strangers.

Molly draped the man's suit coat on the empty chair next to hers.

"I do hope he's back before the presentation begins!" Molly said vaguely to the others at her table. They paid her little attention. Thomas was seated at the table in front of James. Once he'd also faced his chair forward, Molly could see his profile.

As the man at the podium began speaking, Molly pretended to listen but whispered to James, "Meet anyone interesting?"

James took a moment before responding quietly. "No one here is interesting but us."

Molly hid her laugh by taking a sip of water. "Be serious. We need connections. Just this morning a ne'er-do-well dame in a nice hat showed up with a flimsy case, just angling for someone to spy on her husband," Molly murmured. "If I don't find legit cases, that's all I'll be left with. So tell me, did you find anyone *professionally* interesting?"

"Not a one. My friend at the food table was in Parks."

"Parks?"

There was light applause from the crowd as the speaker made some point they all agreed with. James used the sound as cover to speak a bit louder. "Park Safety and Maintenance. Specifically waterways. He sometimes trawls Spreckels and Stow lakes for dumped bodies and stolen goods."

"Well, that could be something!" Molly said quietly as

the sound of the crowd died down again. "Did you get a name?"

"Couldn't," James said. "An unpleasant fellow was speaking loudly nearby about how tonight the city's *vice mongers and perverts* have little time left. I was understandably distracted, and by the time I turned back, my friend had meandered away."

"Vice mongers and perverts? Meaning queers like us?"

"Exactly that," James said. "Us, your friends at Whiskers, the usual band of baddies."

"Whiskers, huh?" Molly stole a look at Thomas seated ahead of her. His wife's hand was resting on his knee.

Molly and James turned their attention to the front of the hall. The man at the podium was none other than Mayor Martin Booker.

"In the years since the Atherton Report, I'm pleased to share that San Francisco's police force has become a beacon of hope for the entirety of the western United States." Mayor Booker's voice boomed through the speakers set up throughout the banquet hall.

Molly smirked. Only a few years prior, while working with Thomas, a private investigator and former Bureau of Investigation agent named Edwin Atherton uncovered the underground workings of San Francisco's gambling and prostitution rings and how they were heavily aided by the police force through bribery.

The Atherton Report indicated that almost one million dollars each year was being paid to police officers and city officials by owners of bootleg gin joints, opium dens, brothels, and gambling houses in exchange for letting them continue to operate in peace. A million dollars' worth of hush money circulating in the pockets of city officials while the rest of the city struggled to buy food, keep their families housed, pay the light bill—it was too much to bear, and the public outcry was great. The findings detailed in the Atherton Report were a stain on the reputation of San Francisco law enforcement. Mayor Booker had been embarrassed to a boiling point, especially since Atherton's investigations made headline news, thanks to the backing of news mogul and anti-vice activist William Randolph Hearst. But at this point, it was believed—hoped, rather—that all officers connected to graft allegations had been expunged.

At the front of the room, Mayor Booker continued. "Though we learned through the experience of prohibition that people's morals and habits cannot be changed by legislation alone, it is my belief, and the belief of the Policeman's Association of San Francisco, that tonight's speaker will finish the work Edwin Atherton started. This new initiative will stamp out any remaining crime that may befoul our city streets—"

"Vice mongers," James whispered.

"—please join me in welcoming Councilman Carl Owens!"

The crowd cheered enthusiastically.

"I know that name," Molly said to James as they clapped.

They watched the councilman make his way up the steps to the podium amid the applause.

"It's the unpleasant fellow!" James whispered urgently.

"It's the ne'er-do-well's husband!" Molly whispered back.

"Who?"

The clapping died down as Carl Owens began to speak.

Molly leaned closer to James. "The woman I told you about who came in this morning. Name's Sylvia Owens. Said her husband Carl was in politics. She also said he put a hit on her."

A woman across the table from Molly heard her whispering and glanced her direction with a look of polite reproach. Molly smiled at her warmly and turned her attention to the front of the hall, biding her time until she could tell James more.

At the front of the room, Carl Owens was wearing a crisp gray suit, cufflinks that sparkled, and a tie clip to match. His dark hair was slicked back in a slightly outdated fashion and made him appear older than Molly suspected he was.

He was almost shouting into the microphone.

"The time for drunks and gamblers, ruffians and louts, hooligans, homosexuals, and hoodlums—*vice mongers, all* —has come to an end!" Carl said. "As head of this initiative, I will lead San Francisco into a newer, cleaner era."

The crowd applauded again and Molly took the opportunity to whisper to James. "The wife's story didn't hold up, not all of it. But she said he's in bed financially with some of these fine officers. Something about exchanging bribes for political favors."

James's eyes opened wide and he arched an eyebrow. "Classic."

There was no time to say more as the noise of the crowd died back again. But now they both listened to Carl's speech with growing interest.

"I count it an honor to work alongside the Policeman's Association of San Francisco," Carl said. "With their support, I will personally shutter every single dark and dirty gathering place of these mongrels that foul our city."

James caught Molly's eye and twirled the tip of one side of his thick mustache: their inside-joke gesture meaning *Whiskers*. Molly stole glances at the faces around them. Some were neutral, but most were smiling. She felt a punch to her gut.

Paula. We have to help.

Carl Owens droned on, citing statistics about gays and lesbians that didn't sound plausible to Molly. She looked at Thomas Parker's profile. He was leaning on his table with his arms crossed, his head slightly down.

His wife turned toward him with a soft smile and said something to him quietly. He nodded and briefly gave her what to Molly looked like a forced smile. Molly watched as Thomas took a deep breath and looked at the faces around him, just as Molly had just done.

Did he know about this? Molly wondered. *He can't be supporting this.*

As Carl spoke, Molly ran through what Sylvia had told her earlier that morning. It was clear she had been spitballing her story. Nothing she'd said made sense. She didn't have a case or even a plausible lie. But it was clear that Sylvia didn't like her husband.

Maybe the feeling was mutual.

Even so, Molly couldn't tell if Carl was the kind of man to put a hit on his wife. In any case, why bother putting a hit on her at all? Why not simply give her a miserable life while he did what he wanted? Like most husbands Molly had heard about.

Molly thought of the way Sylvia had stood so close to her in the office. When Sylvia had locked onto Molly's gaze, she seemed to plumb her depths. Molly remembered the smell of powder and cigarette smoke that had come into the room with her. And there was something else —lilacs.

Molly remembered when Sylvia had grasped her hands… *No.* She couldn't let her mind go there. Whatever Sylvia wanted, it wasn't that. And if she did, Sylvia was bad news. Molly knew better than to get tangled up in a situation like that…*again.*

One way or another, Sylvia was trouble. Just the kind of woman Molly couldn't stay away from. Or she would have been, back when she still made room in her life for women.

Molly watched Carl orating at the podium to his rapt audience. His face got redder as he became more emphatic. He occasionally smoothed his hair back as he spoke. For a brief moment, Molly imagined Sylvia and Carl in bed together…and immediately stopped. The picture was dreadful.

"I'm especially proud to be working so closely with the

vice squad on this project," Carl Owens said from the front of the room. "My esteemed colleague Chief Lonnie King will be overseeing the procedural events of the initiative." The police chief had been sitting near the podium. At the mention of his name, he rose and gave a slight bow to the audience. He was a stout, middle-aged man who looked every bit the part of a chief of police. "Chief King and I have worked diligently on this plan, which we have already begun executing. We've spent long hours developing a methodical approach to our mission and are confident in our vision for success. Vice men, I am so pleased to be working with you on this project. Would each of you please stand and receive your applause?"

Around the room, a dozen men rose from their seats at the tables scattered throughout the banquet hall. They wore suits of charcoal gray or navy blue. Some gave a small wave to the clapping crowd. From their seats next to them, their wives looked on in proud admiration.

Then, at the table in front of James, Detective Thomas Parker swiftly rose up from his seat. Molly's breath caught at the sight of him. He stood unmoving, with his back to her, not waving or seeming to even notice the spirited cheers from around the room.

At the conclusion of Carl Owen's speech, there was a partial standing ovation. Now that the speaking portion of the evening was over, the crowd began mingling as music swelled through the speakers again. The event was scheduled to last for another hour or so. Molly grabbed the suit jacket from the back of the empty chair next to her. "Oh, dear me, I do hope he didn't wander off drunk somewhere!" she said to no one.

Molly milled about for a few moments, hoping to catch Thomas's eye again, to learn what she could just by the way he might look at her, but he'd vanished into the crowd.

Outside, Molly met James in the side alley.

"I need you in the office Monday morning," Molly said, hooking her fictional husband's jacket over one shoulder.

"I had a feeling you'd say that," James said.

They walked slowly toward their parked cars as they spoke in low voices. The moonlight shone down through gaps between buildings as the soft warmth of the summer evening clung to the brick around them. "Maybe Carl Owens isn't the kind of man to put a hit on his wife. But he is slimy. And we can't let him get away with what he's doing," Molly said.

"He's not completely in the wrong," James said with a reproachful look. "After all, places like Whiskers—well, they *are* illegal after all, even without Paula's family being what they are. The way he described his plan...Molly, he has the law on his side. I know how injustice fires you up. But everything he mentioned about this plan of his is perfectly legal."

As they spoke, Molly took off her costume glasses and jewelry. They stopped at Molly's car where she perched in the front seat and removed the itchy wig, giving her scalp a much-needed scratching. She released her pinned up curls that had been trapped in the hot wig for hours.

She tossed the wig unceremoniously in the passenger seat. "Not if he's involved in some kind of political bribery and police corruption. After the Atherton Report, Booker blew his lid about keeping the police force in check. If there is still something underhanded happening behind closed doors, the mayor would have a fit. James, this could be big for us!"

James paused in front of his car. "You won't make a lot of friends in the police department to give you case referrals if you're simultaneously investigating them. What happened to networking?"

"Just come to the office Monday morning, James. Please? Sylvia will be calling, and we can dig into this case."

"*Sylvia*, is it?" James smirked at Molly. "And in the meantime?"

"In the meantime, I have to break into the police station." Molly gave James a fierce, brief hug, then turned over her engine.

James was aghast. "The police station! What do you…when?"

"Right now," Molly said. "See you Monday morning. Give my love to Lewis!"

CHAPTER
FIVE

Breaking into the police station wasn't the impossible feat it should have been. For one thing, as a former employee of the San Francisco Police Department, Molly already knew her way around the building. It being late on a hot, sleepy night, the station would be relatively quiet, making it much easier to sneak in and out than any other day of the week. Of course, a police station in a large city wouldn't be completely empty, no matter the time of day or night. But with most of the police force still celebrating at the banquet in city hall, now was the perfect time to act.

The physical act of breaking into a building didn't faze her. Molly knew she could break into or out of most any building, safe, or locked door. It wasn't the gross mechanics of the thing that posed the most challenge. It was the required finesse. It was being sure to leave no trail behind her. It was about knowing the right time to act, not a moment too early or too late. And sometimes that meant a last-minute break-in. Like tonight. It was for these moment's-notice occasions that Molly kept a diverse collection of disguises, costumes, and breaking-and-entering supplies in the trunk of her car at all times.

In Carl Owens's grandiose speech at the banquet, he promised to crack down on illegal establishments such as gay clubs. Since Carl named Chief Lonnie King as his co-conspirator on this project, Molly imagined his office could be a good place to start looking for a paper trail. She'd never worked with Chief King. The man who had been police chief when Molly worked with Thomas had retired not long after Molly and Thomas parted ways, and King had moved up into the position from another department. In any case, Molly knew where the chief's office was. And she knew how to get in.

She'd discovered a secret way through the police station when she'd been filing forged documents installing James as the owner of her detective agency. Now, she was ready to see if those secret paths were still available.

Though she'd initially shrugged off Sylvia Owens's case, Carl's speech at the banquet made Molly curious as to his nature. Even if it turned out there was nothing to Sylvia's story, Molly knew she'd need to stop Carl from making good on his plan to close down spaces like Whiskers.

But hunches and secondhand rumors won't be enough, Molly realized. She would need direct evidence of Carl's misdeeds in order to have any hope of making a dent in his plans. And she knew just who she'd take her evidence to once she had it. She wasn't sure what she was looking for, only that she'd know it when she saw it.

Directing her Mercury Town Sedan into the underground parking garage of the station gave Molly an unexpected feeling of mournful nostalgia. It had been only about a year since she'd stopped working at the station, but it seemed like ages ago. The parking lot was as familiar as an old friend. She'd come through this lot hundreds of times during her time working as Thomas's secretary: from those thrilling first cases, through the bitter hurt of Thomas's betrayal, to her eventual decision to leave the police department.

Molly recalled the anxiety she felt when she eventually filled out the application and paid her fee to become a private investigator herself. She then used the document forging tricks she learned while working on fraud cases with Thomas to create a similar, though fraudulent, license for James. She'd told herself that since James wasn't doing any detective work of his own, his forged papers caused no one any harm. Still, she felt a subtle fluttering of nerves in her gut when she thought of those forged papers on file in the storeroom.

There were only a few cars in the lot this late in the evening. Molly parked in a dark corner. She finally peeled off the uncomfortable woolen dress and swiftly swapped it for a new look scrounged from the trunk of her car.

Looking into the reflection of her car windows, she inspected her work. She wore a pair of men's coveralls, men's work boots, and an oversized floppy cap. She'd tucked her hair into the cap and shrugged. *Close enough.*

Molly hoped it was too dark for anyone who might be around to take a close look at her anyway. Lastly, she grabbed her toolbox from the trunk of her car.

She walked through the dim garage toward the service elevator. The sound of her work boots reverberated softly against the cement walls and steel beams, though they made much less sound than her high-heeled oxfords would have.

At the service elevator, Molly pulled a screwdriver from the toolbox. A quick glance around the quiet and dim parking garage told her she was alone. She quickly unscrewed the thin metal panel near the elevator's doors.

Years before, she'd seen an elevator mechanic open this panel to tinker with the inner workings of the elevator when they'd gotten jammed up somehow. Molly had watched the mechanic at work under the pretense of casual conversation about the weather.

The elevator was not for use by regular staff members or citizens. It was supposed to only be used by delivery-men, some higher-ranking officers, and for occasional pris-oner transport. As such, the elevator couldn't be operated without a key, which Molly didn't have.

But as she learned from watching the mechanic, if you opened the panel and flipped a switch, you didn't need a key. Seemed like a pretty flimsy security system. But since it worked in her favor, she'd make use of it.

After flipping the bypass switch, she pressed the button for the third floor. The mechanical gears sprang to life and Molly rode in silence through the dead center of the police station.

The doors opened on the third floor of the building, where many of the administrative offices were. The main ceiling lights were shut off, but a few late-working officers sat at desks with table lamps. The yellowish pools of light illuminated the paperwork, files, and photos that littered their desks.

At the sound of the elevator doors opening, one officer looked up from his work. Molly pretended to thoroughly investigate the paper on the clipboard she carried, then looked around the room briefly, as though searching for a specific room. The only offices on this floor were positioned around the perimeter of the building, with the center filled with rows of desks for the officers and secretaries. In her secretary days, Molly had worked on a different floor, but they were all laid out the same.

After a slight show of comparing office numbers and names to the blank piece of paper on her clipboard, Molly walked purposefully toward the police chief's office. She glanced at the open desks again and saw the one officer still watching her, curious. Confidence was key. She gave a slight wave with a wrench in her hand and kept walking. The officer gave a nod back and then turned back to his work.

Thankfully, the chief's door was unlocked. Lock-picking was easy, but it's another thing to do it while someone is watching. And something else altogether when the door belonged to the chief of police.

Once safely inside Lonnie King's office, Molly closed the door behind her. The windows that faced the inside of the building were covered with closed blinds. For now, Molly could work in peace.

Chief King's office had large windows that offered a picturesque cityscape. The lights from the city brightened up the room enough that Molly didn't need to switch on a lamp. A large, squat desk sat in front of the windows. Molly scanned the top of it. Like the other officers' desks in the open room, Lonnie's desk was covered in papers, files, notecards, and other detritus of police work.

Nothing she rifled through told her anything. On a hunch, Molly lifted the large leather desk pad that spanned most of the surface area of the desk. She was careful to avoid disturbing the papers that were strewn about on top.

Underneath the desk pad, Molly found a thin file folder containing a mimeographed handwritten list of addresses and letters:

410 Eddy St.

2504 Fillmore St.

529 Folsom St.

516 N. Green St.

There were a dozen or so addresses on the list. The two at the top—on Eddy and Fillmore streets—were crossed out with a neat pencil line.

With a frown, Molly wondered what it all meant, whispering to herself, "Five-sixteen Green Street...is that...?" *Whiskers is on Green Street.* She pulled a small notebook and pencil from her pocket and quickly copied the list, filling up three and a half of the tiny pages.

Mindful of the officer who'd seen her enter the office,

she rushed to put the original list back into the folder and then slid the folder back into place under the desk pad. Upon exiting Lonnie's office, Molly geared up to offer a deep-voiced *goodnight* to the officer who'd been working late. But he—along with the other officers—had already left, so Molly escaped without incident.

Back in the parking garage, she reset the key bypass switch and replaced the panel, carefully tightening each corner screw.

Aside from the possible address for Whiskers, Molly didn't recognize any of the other addresses, but she knew Folsom Street was in the Mission. Maybe it was the address for the Hot Spot. Still, a lead was a lead, no matter how small. Molly decided that come Monday, she would track down the Hot Spot's owner—Paula's friend—and learn more about what had him so concerned.

CHAPTER
SIX

Before Carl Owens left for the policeman's banquet, Sylvia had locked herself in her second-floor bedroom. She'd planned a story for Carl to beg off having to attend the event—a headache, a cough, a fever.

But there was no need. As Carl got dressed for the evening, he'd only berated her through her closed bedroom door: "I'd expect you to spoil the whole thing anyway. Moping around like you do. I'm very important to these people, you know. They're all gathering to hear what I have to say. And everyone will cheer for it, I'm sure. Everyone but *you*, I'd suppose. And no one wants to see some moping *woman* who isn't happy for her husband on a night like this."

His cruel words simply slid off her without inflicting any of the intended damage. Tonight, she'd have a few blessed hours to herself. That's all Sylvia cared about. Time was all she needed to continue her search.

After leaving the detective's office that morning, Sylvia was even more determined to put an end to Carl's plans. The secretary—was her name Molly?—had indicated that Sylvia's case might not have legs. And she couldn't blame her. Sylvia kicked herself that she hadn't prepared a better story. She hated that it sounded so flimsy. But how could she get anyone to help her if she told them *all* the torrid and true details?

Were you able to fight him off?

The secretary's question had thrown her. Sylvia was no great brute, just of average build for a woman. Even without knowing anything about the supposed attacker, it was a hard sell that Sylvia would have been able to fight off anyone, let alone a man in a rage. But telling the truth —that she'd been simply threatened by a man she knew— wasn't going to make anyone rush to the rescue.

The fact is, he *had* threatened her. And his threats were made all the more horrifying by what he'd said about Jane. "Carl should have taken care of you like I did with Jane," he'd growled with a menacing look Sylvia knew well.

In any case, it didn't much matter what someone's secretary thought. As long as she passed along the information to the detective, Sylvia was sure he would help. She could explain it all to him. But first she needed more evidence. So with Carl out of the house for a few hours, Sylvia got to work.

As Sylvia had learned throughout her fifteen years with Carl, she could never tell what sort of mood he'd be in. Sometimes he barely spoke to her. Other times, he'd grill her for days about her goings-on. Where was she going, who would she be with, how long would she be gone, why couldn't he go with her? As though anything she did out of his sight was suspicious.

Usually, Sylvia just needed to get out of the house, go for a walk through the neighborhood or the park, or meander through her favorite stores—not for the vapid reason of shopping just to shop, but just to do something out of the house. To get away from Carl.

Sylvia began telling Carl she had a salon appointment, which often shut him up. The first time she knew she could use this excuse was one evening when Sylvia had come home after an afternoon of blithely strolling through the park and reading her book. Carl was already home from city hall when she'd arrived. He said, "Your hair looks better that way. They should do it like that every time." He'd assumed she'd gotten home from the salon, though she'd never mentioned anything of the sort and hadn't been to the salon in weeks. It became a game to her then, to see how little attention he paid to her. It was the only thing she could do to keep her sanity.

Until she met Jane.

Once Sylvia heard Carl leave for the evening, she hurried into his office.

Light from the setting sun cast an orange glow throughout the space. The papers on his desk were tidier than they'd been the other day. She was looking for the document he'd been working on. After tonight, when his city cleanup plans had been announced, there would be momentum toward that future imagined time when Carl planned to make an even bigger speech. A speech he'd give after doing something quite dreadful. A speech he'd been working on for ages. But Sylvia vowed to do everything in her power to stop him.

She longed to take all the papers she'd seen on Carl's desk into the detective's office. But of course, if Carl had discovered them missing, she'd be in for it. She had to look again, just to be sure there wasn't something else she'd missed. Even something small she could bring to the detective that would clearly show what Carl was up to.

After sifting through a few papers and files and finding nothing of interest, she tried for a drawer. Opening the bottom right-hand drawer, Sylvia saw the usual jumbled stack of papers and files. But what was perched on top of the pile made her hands tremble.

A letter addressed to her—no, *two* letters. *Three*!

Three envelopes read *Mrs. Sylvia Owens* with her and Carl's address in a careful script. When Sylvia saw the return address—the same on each envelope—she let out a sound that was part gasp, part shriek. "She's *alive*?" she asked the empty room.

Each envelope sported a ragged open edge, presumably from Carl inspecting them before hiding them in the drawer. Sylvia felt a sickly chill at the thought of Carl reading them before she even knew they existed. But no matter now.

She settled onto the floor near the desk and gathered the letters on her lap. Two of the envelopes had been postmarked two years prior, separated by a few months. That would have been just after they'd last seen each other.

Knowing that Jane was alive lifted a weight from

Sylvia's chest that she'd carried for so long. *I thought for sure…* But she refused to even finish the thought. She read the letters in the order they'd come, hoping to piece together a story about where Jane had gone, what happened to her, and what she might be going through.

But with a maddening dullness, the letters droned on about the weather, a trip to the seaside, musings about what Christmas gifts Jane might get for her sisters. The contents were disappointing and bland. Jane wrote nothing of consequence. No answers as to what she might have been thinking. No neatly wrapped conclusion to what they'd been through. The letters could have been written by someone's spinster grandmother to a distant cousin—kind, but lacking vitality or personal connection. Sylvia replaced both letters in their envelopes, feeling the loneliness creep back in. If Jane wouldn't even acknowledge what they'd gone through, or give her any clues as to where she was now, then Sylvia was alone in her fight.

But the third letter seemed to have arrived only this past week. The postmark read *9 AUG 1943* in crisp red ink. With nearly two years separating the letters, surely this most recent letter would provide some insight.

Sylvia grasped the envelope, willing herself to not be disappointed by the contents, whatever they were. There was a spot of ink in the word *San* that had gotten smudged from someone's greasy or wet fingerprint somewhere along its journey. Sylvia parted the open edges of the envelope, pulled out the letter, and carefully unfolded it.

While the other letters were each a single page with

neat script on both sides, this most recent letter was much shorter, taking up only a few sparse lines:

Dear Sylvia,

I'm back in town and need to see you. I've missed you so much. Meet me at the Hot Spot next Monday night.

I have so much to tell you.

Love, Jane

She's missed me? Back in town? These few words brought up so many questions. In any case, all that mattered was that Jane was alright after all. In a moment of quick thinking, Sylvia folded a few blank sheets of paper and slid them into each envelope, keeping the actual letters for herself. She then retreated from Carl's office.

So that was that. She'd have a chance to talk to Jane in only a couple of nights. Maybe they could be friends again. *Unlikely.* Maybe Jane would help her with the detective. *Doubtful.* In any case, she'd get to learn what had happened after they'd last seen each other.

As she applied cold cream to her face, Sylvia imagined what it would be like to be at the Hot Spot with Jane again, after so many years.

CHAPTER
SEVEN

The morning after the policeman's banquet, James sat at his kitchen table with a glass of orange juice and a cup of coffee in front of him. He gingerly sipped the juice but hadn't yet touched his coffee. The appetizers he'd snacked on throughout the evening had given him indigestion.

"How about pancakes, then?" James's partner Lewis asked him. "I won't have you skipping breakfast, you know."

James smiled, obligingly. "I will eat pancakes, just for you."

Lewis set a small cup of pink liquid in front of James and kissed the top of his head. "This will help too."

James downed the chalky medicine while Lewis disappeared into the kitchen. Spreading the *San Francisco Gazette* in front of him, he scanned the paper through his reading glasses.

The news of the day was nothing remarkable. *I should*

get Lewis a new hat for his birthday. A Brooks Brothers ad promised the finest in straw Panama hats for $3.85. It was a bit steep for a hat, but Lewis deserved it. As if to drive this point home, another small box in the corner of the *Gazette* advertised the latest production Lewis's theater company was working on: *Follies from the Front,* an original musical Lewis had written based on the more joyful times together with their unit in the war. Of course, the family-friendly show omitted any notion of James and Lewis's romance.

The warm, sweet smell of pancakes made James's belly rumble. Perhaps he was hungry after all this morning. Lewis's cooking always had a way of making him feel better.

Over the years they'd been together, James and Lewis had fallen into an easy routine. Most afternoons and evenings, Lewis worked at the theater, usually running lights and doing technical work for the small productions. It was because of Lewis's technical know-how that Molly's signal system was set up properly in the detective office. The switches in the desk and the lights over the office door were an idea Lewis and Molly had come up with when Molly convinced James to help her with the agency. And since then, those red and green lights flashing above the door had appeared in not a few of James's more anxiety-ridden dreams.

For practicality reasons, James knew the arrangement was a good one. James made forty percent of everything Molly raked in—far more than he made in the small theater circuit he and Lewis had traveled once they'd returned from the war. At times, he did enjoy the social experiment of playacting the role of a private detective on a real-world stage.

Suddenly, a small headline in the middle pages of the newspaper caught his attention: "Search Continues for Pacific Heights Restauranteur."

There was a sudden clenching in his chest. The restauranteur in question was an old friend of theirs. Gene owned an Italian restaurant called Gino's Restaurant and Bar in Pacific Heights, a place James and Lewis went to once every few months, along with other gay men and lesbians, as well as unsuspecting straight couples. While Gino's wasn't specifically a queer joint, those who preferred to keep a lower profile would visit occasionally, imagining they appeared to be business partners, or old college friends, or brothers or sisters who were catching up over a nice, quiet meal.

Until a few weeks ago, when Gene disappeared. And none of the cooks or waitstaff knew where he'd gone, so Gino's had remained closed.

"They still haven't found Gene," James called to Lewis. His voice sounded as weary as he felt.

Lewis leaned through the kitchen doorframe, a metal spatula in one hand. He looked at James for a moment, then opened his mouth to speak. A sob came out instead.

"Fuck," James said softly. He stood and hugged Lewis, tight.

"He didn't just disappear," Lewis said into James's shoulder.

"I know."

"He wouldn't do that."

"I know, honey," James said. "But you know how he likes to travel. Maybe he skipped town to go somewhere. Maybe…he's just taking a longer trip than usual."

Still holding onto James, Lewis shook his head. "Without telling anyone?"

James faltered, searching for comforting words he himself doubted. "Well, you know how he is. He likes to get lost. We haven't talked to him for months anyway. We don't know what's going on with him. Maybe he fell in love with a handsome Italian man and is out there living the high life."

After a moment, Lewis pulled back from the embrace and slipped back into the kitchen while wiping his eyes. "My pancakes are burning."

As soon as James sat down and turned back to his paper, there was a knock at the door.

Finding a bright-eyed Molly Malone standing on his porch, James couldn't help but grin softly with a shake of his head. "Why am I not surprised?"

Molly gave him a pat on the shoulder as she brushed past him into the row house. "Good morning to my favorite boys!"

"Is that Molly?" Lewis called from the kitchen.

"It is I, my sweet!" Molly took her coat off. "Your second favorite person after that old grump."

James allowed himself a soft laugh. "She's blessing our Sunday breakfast with her uninvited presence." At least Molly could lighten the mood. Lewis wouldn't want to be so down with Molly around.

Lewis emerged from the kitchen and squeezed Molly in a hug. His eyes were red, but James saw that he'd managed to find a genuinely happy smile. Lewis had always loved Molly. "She's always invited, James!" Lewis headed for the kitchen. "Coffee, Molly?"

"Not for me, thanks," Molly answered. "I've had enough this morning. Already can't keep up with my own thoughts."

James resumed his seat at the table and folded up his paper while Lewis set out syrup, butter, jam, and fruit. "Will you be joining us for breakfast, then?" Lewis asked. "I didn't know to expect you," he said with a frown.

"I know. I'm sorry, Lew!" Molly said. "No breakfast for me. I won't be long. I just need to talk to James for a moment. Happy anniversary, by the way!"

"Thank you," Lewis said with a slight bow. "I'll forgive you for stealing James last night if you'll take me out to lunch soon. I've missed you, dear."

"I would adore taking you to lunch, Lew. See how nice he treats me?" Molly turned to James. "Why don't you love me that much?"

James gave her a reproachful look. "We are eating breakfast in fifteen minutes. You'll either join us and we'll done talking about work, or you'll be gone by then."

"I'll be gone," Molly said.

"I'll leave you *vice mongers* to it, then," Lewis said with a wink.

Molly laughed. "James told you!"

"It's my new favorite phrase!" Lewis exclaimed. "I'll make it into a needlepoint pillow. We should open our own bar and call it Vice Mongers." He left the room with a laugh, returning to the kitchen to finish breakfast.

As much as a quiet morning without Molly's antics sounded nice, James was grateful for the lighthearted mood her presence brought. Especially now.

"What is it, boss?" James asked, removing his glasses.

"First of all, the key part of *private detective* is the *private* part," Molly chided.

"Who's talking about *private parts*?" Lewis called from the kitchen, laughing again.

James couldn't help but smile at that one. "I'm not a private detective, Molly. You are. I'm only a paid actor with forged papers you were so kind to file away somewhere."

"Right you are, my friend," Molly said. "Which is just why I'm here. I need you in the office tomorrow. A lady will be calling and I need you to get the scoop."

"*A lady*, is it? Do you mean *Carl Owen's wife*?"

"Yes."

"The 'ne'er-do-well'?" James squinted at her as he considered. "You've decided to take her case?"

Molly shook her head. "I wouldn't say that, exactly. The case she tried to bring me still doesn't make sense. I don't know what her angle is. But if Councilman Owens uses his wallet to get people to do what he wants, then he's not likely a *brute force* kind of guy. It's usually one or the other. But if there is a financial exchange happening between Carl Owens and the San Francisco Police Department, I want to know about it. I found something interesting in Chief King's office last night and I've got to talk to Paula about it. Is Carl Owens out to murder his wife? I don't think so. But his political plans include shutting down places like Whiskers, and I can't let that happen. This is a pure bribery case—graft at its finest. I'm gathering what evidence I can to take to Booker."

James took a gulp of juice. The medicine had already begun to settle his belly. "Why the mayor? He had nothing but glowing praise for the initiative. What makes you think he'd care?"

"Because they're going behind his back. Or at least, I think they are. In any case, Booker stands to be made a fool of. Whether he thinks Carl Owens's plan is a good idea or not—*vice mongers* or not—he'll look weak if the police force he just cleaned up with Atherton is still up to its old tricks. Booker will help. I know he will." Molly finally slowed and took a breath. "So. Can I count on you to be there tomorrow?"

Molly looked expectantly at James. The determined look on her face always made it so difficult to say no. On the other hand, James was tired.

"I'll be honest with you, Molly," he said. "I'm about ready to retire."

"You're not that old!" Molly laughed and plucked a few red grapes from the bowl in the center of the breakfast table. "Besides, you need the money."

"I don't, actually." His voice quieted. "Lewis just picked up more work at the theater—his show, remember? And I'll be performing in the production after that one." He looked frankly at Molly until he had her attention. Her smirk faltered. "This whole line of work is weighing me down, and—"

"I know," Molly jumped in, speaking quickly. James could almost see her physically shrug off his words. "Everything has been so last minute lately. I should give you more of a heads up about things. And I will. I'll *try*. But when something comes up, we need to act fast."

James glanced toward the kitchen where Lewis continued softly bustling about. "It's not just the schedule. It's the rest of my life too. Look, I was happy to help you get started with the agency. I just can't keep doing it. And I don't want to slow you down. But I also can't be…well, a *puppet* anymore."

Molly's face fell. "What about Whiskers? It's where we met!"

A brief flash of memory brought James back to the night he and Lewis met Molly, about five years prior. Lewis and Molly had struck up a conversation at the bar, and before James knew it, Lewis had invited Molly over for brunch the next day. That was when James was thirty-two, the same age as Molly now. Though by that time, he'd begun to get worn out on the social scene of the underground clubs. Yet Molly seemed in no rush to slow her nightlife. "We're not big bar-goers anymore these days."

"Bar-goers! James, it's all we have. It's not about whether you find the environment appealing or not. Who cares if you don't like going to bars? It's our community. It's the only place we can gather—to feel *normal*."

James was silent for a moment, then shrugged. "If going to bars every night is what it takes to be part of this community, then I guess we're not part of it. I'm much better off without spending evenings sneaking into dark places and keeping to the shadows. It's terribly exhausting. Pair that with lying during the day while I'm working with you…it's just all too much. Lewis and I have been together since our twenties. We did the bars, the parties, the occasional jail time. It *was* fun. But now…we're in a different stage of our lives. It's just not about the bars for us anymore."

Molly looked out the big bay window to the bright day outside. "Some of us need spaces like that, James. Which is why it would be devastating if they were shut down."

Lewis entered from the kitchen, carrying a stack of pancakes and a pitcher of juice. "He's telling you, isn't he?" Lewis looked at Molly with kind eyes. He set the food down, then sat at the table next to James. James took Lewis's hand in his.

Molly took a moment before responding. James saw her mulling over the facts. He knew Molly believed she couldn't work without the image of him behind the detective's desk. *I just can't take much more of it.*

"I need a little more time. To get my feet under me," Molly said. "Please help me figure this thing out—whatever is happening with Carl Owens—and after that…I'll let you go. And I'll do it on my own. I just need your help with this last one, James. This one isn't just a *job*, it's about our *lives*. Or mine, anyway."

James looked at Lewis and then rubbed his eyes. He took a breath before speaking. "I'll be there tomorrow. I won't leave you high and dry. But I'm not in it for much longer. I can't be."

Molly paused briefly, considering this. "I can't thank you enough," she finally said.

James smiled, hoping to break the tension. "I'm still waiting on that bottle of champagne you promised."

"I'll make it two."

Lewis began setting out plates. "Stay for pancakes?"

She shook her head, standing up and gathering her coat. "Thank you, my sweet, but no. I've got lots to do." Molly buttoned her coat. "I'll show myself out. James, I'll see you tomorrow. And thank you again."

James sat behind his stack of pancakes, slightly reeling from Molly's usual whirlwind of energy.

Lewis kissed the top of James's head. "I'm proud of you for telling her."

CHAPTER
EIGHT

In the office the next morning, Molly sat across from James, both of them waiting in stilted silence for Sylvia's call. Molly could read on James's face that he wasn't pleased with being there. His comment yesterday morning about retiring had jarred her. But he was right. She needed to do this without him. Right after the Owens case.

Last week at this time, Molly was just wrapping up the Underwood case, finalizing her notes and compiling the report for James to hand over to the client. It seemed like a hundred years had passed between then and now. The Bert Underwood job was just *a job*—for the sake of a paycheck, doing what she loved, the thrill of the work.

The Owens job wasn't really even a job. Molly wasn't sure who, if anyone, would be cutting her a check once the work was completed. For the first time, she didn't care about the money. The work in front of her now was a matter of principle, of right and wrong. A way to give back to her beloved community. Regardless of what happened with her business—if James decided to quit and she had to figure out a way to make it on her own—she knew she would see this thing through to the end. Whatever that was.

"What time did she say?" James asked. He had a newspaper spread in front of him, a cup of coffee cooling on the desk. Molly sat in the armchair in the corner of James's office. For the first hour of the morning, she'd placed herself in the front room at the secretary's desk, anticipating Sylvia's call at any moment. But as the morning stretched into midday, no call came.

"I told her to call after nine."

Both James and Molly looked at the clock on the wall above the bookshelves. It was almost half past eleven. "*Molly.*" The annoyance in his voice finished the rest of the sentence for him.

"I know," she said. "I'm sorry! She was pretty urgent about the whole thing Saturday morning. I don't know why she would drop it all of a sudden."

"Can you call her?"

"She said not to call at home. Because of Carl."

James sighed heavily. "But won't he be at work? Midday on a Monday?"

"Yeah…"

"If this isn't happening today, I have other things I could be doing."

"I know," Molly said. "Alright. We'll call."

"Me or you?"

Molly thought for a moment. "I'll do it. If Carl answers

I can be…a lady from the salon or a clothing boutique calling about an order. If he heard a man's voice asking for Sylvia, he might become suspicious."

"Works for me, boss." James turned back to his newspaper as Molly returned to the front room of the office.

She pulled out the small notebook she'd used to make notes and found that she hadn't even taken down Sylvia's number. *Sylvia Owens, issue uncertain, possible marital issues, politician husband Carl, fearful of working with law enforcement.*

Her notes seemed so simple compared to what she'd learned in the few days since. She'd forgotten that Sylvia hadn't given her phone number at all. Of course, Sylvia herself had been quite a distraction.

Molly turned to the thick phone book stashed in the bottom drawer of her desk. She flipped to the O's, scanning the pages until she came to several dozen *Owens* listings. There were two listings for *Owens, C.* The first one she called was an elderly woman, Clarice, who lived alone and had no knowledge of a Carl or Sylvia Owens. The second number rang several times before Molly finally hung up.

"James," she called through to the other room. "You can go home for the day. I'm sorry for the wasted morning."

After James left the office, Molly felt his annoyance clouding her mood as well. *Dammit, Sylvia. Where are you?* For a moment, she wondered if she should feel concern. After all, Sylvia had said someone tried to attack her. But when pressed, her details hadn't made sense. *What isn't she telling me, and why?*

In any case, Molly couldn't reach her by phone and the phonebook didn't list a home address she could visit. Molly decided she could at least hang around the office and wait for Sylvia's call on her own.

After all, there wasn't much else for her to do until later in the evening. By then, the Hot Spot would be open and she could talk with Paula's friend.

CHAPTER
NINE

Across town from the detective office on Ohlone Street, Detective Thomas Parker sat at his desk in the police station, ruminating on Molly Malone. They hadn't spoken in over a year. Since they'd been professionally close, it pained him terribly the way he'd left things—forcing her to transfer departments like that. But he couldn't take the risk that she'd talk. He had a wife and kids to consider.

Seeing her in Whiskers the other day, and then again at the policeman's banquet—it all came rushing back. Somehow he'd avoided seeing her for a year, but it was only a matter of time before their paths crossed again. And now that they had, he wasn't sure about his next move.

He just wanted things to go back to normal, how they used to be. He could do his work on the force, spend a few quiet evenings a week in the gay clubs, but always make sure to return to his wife and kids at the end of it all. Seeing Molly Malone again suggested that wasn't possible.

She was fun, smart, friendly. But sometimes Molly's drive and single-minded focus created headaches for others.

There was a rock in Thomas's gut he couldn't ignore. Molly always seemed to have a way of complicating things for him.

As he reflected on his former friendship with Molly, Thomas watched Chief Lonnie King walk into the middle of the floor where many officer's desks were lined up in neat rows. Chief King put a foot up on an empty chair. That was his sign he was about to make an announcement.

"Alright girls, listen up," he bellowed. "We've got a town to clean up and I need your cooperation. I need each and every one of you tonight for a bust at one of the fairy joints." Around him, Thomas's colleagues grinned, and some let out a *whoop* of excitement. The rock in Thomas's belly got bigger.

"We'll meet back here tonight at eleven to get rallied up. Then we'll bust around midnight. Don't worry about playing too soft on this crowd. You heard what Booker said in his little speech. We got city officials on our side for this one, so go as hard as you like."

Thomas focused on keeping his face neutral while he wondered which of the city's gay bars he would have a hand in shutting down in a few short hours.

Packed into the back of a paddy wagon with his fellow officers, Thomas lit a cigarette. He still wasn't sure where they were headed, but he watched out the window in anticipation.

"…she had 'em out to *here*, no foolin'," the young officer sitting next to Thomas was saying. Hank was new, a few months out of the academy. Thomas recognized the enthusiasm and drive for power in this young officer. He'd once had it himself. As the wagon bumped along its route, the officers gave young Hank the spotlight he so enjoyed. Hank was filling them in on a whorehouse raid he'd been on a few weeks prior. Since the vice men didn't work the same stings, they often regaled each other with detailed accounts of what the others had missed.

Hank laughed loudly at his own story, among the lascivious grins of his fellow officers. "Too bad it's shut down now, or I'd have gone back to visit her myself!"

From the opposite corner of the dark wagon, a gruff voice emerged: "Trixie's ain't shut." It was Pete, an experienced vice man of many years.

The smile dropped from Hank's face and a frown replaced it. "It ain't shut? Pete, you were there. We shut the place down. Those girls sat right here in this wagon. We shut the whole place down."

More officers grinned, looking back now toward Pete, knowing where this was going.

As the vehicle turned onto a side street, the passing streetlights swung around to illuminate each officer's face in turn. The wagon cruised along the cooling and quiet streets, and Thomas watched the buildings pass by. He gripped the edge of the hard metal seat beneath him. He recognized more buildings. He guessed where the wagon was headed now.

"We shut Trixie's for the *night,* my boy," said Pete in his deep voice. "Maybe a week, tops. She's open again."

The other officers shot their attention back to Hank. Thomas watched their faces, eager for the lesson Hank was about to get.

Hank shook his head. "How can they do that? We'll close 'em again!"

"Not if they keep up their end of the bargain," Pete said.

Despite himself, Thomas watched too, curious how Hank would take the news.

"What bargain?" Hank asked. He looked at the grins of his fellow officers, understanding now that they knew something he didn't. His cheeks turned pink with embarrassment.

"It's all capitalism, son," Pete's gravelly baritone thundered in the wagon with his laugh. "Like taxes. They slip us a percentage and we leave 'em to their business. If anyone should forget to pay or neighbors start complaining..." Pete shrugged. "We make a show of arrests until they make it right."

"But that's *bribery.* What about Atherton?" Hank sat up tall. Thomas inclined away from him as much as he could on his edge of the seat.

"What about him?" another officer piped up. The others nodded and laughed off the name.

Pete answered. "Edwin Atherton gave his little snitch report, picked up his check, and skipped town. He don't run the show anymore. Booker cleared house as best he could. Which means anyone still on the force from before Atherton knows how to keep our noses clean."

The other officers grunted in approval, proud of this accomplishment. Thomas avoided anyone's attempt at eye contact in that moment.

Pete went on. "Nothing's changed. These places we shut down? Once the heat's off, their customers crawl back like cockroaches. Cockroaches with *money*. So yeah, of course Trixie's is open again. They're open right now, in fact. We can go tonight after we bust the fairies. Tell you what—" Pete reached into his pocket and pulled out some bills. "Tonight, Trixie's is on me. Let's make a man out of you, kid! And tell her I said hello."

More laughs. Hank frowned, looking like he wasn't sure if he should take the money or not. Thomas snubbed out his cigarette and anticipated the next turn the vehicle might make. If they made a right on the next street, and then an immediate left, he'd know for sure.

Ultimately, Hank ignored Pete's outstretched bills. "So what about the queers, then? Are they going to open up again too?"

Thomas felt the disgust in Hank's question and the rock in his gut became a boulder. He took a deep breath to steady himself, turning his face to the breeze that flowed through the open grates of the paddy windows. There it was: 529 Folsom Street, the dingy corner entrance of the Hot Spot, one of the gay bars he'd visited many times over the years. Last time he was there was only a few weeks ago, with Joseph.

Thomas's pulse raced as he felt the wagon begin to slow its momentum. Along with all the other officers in the wagon, he looked at Pete to get his take on Hank's question.

Pete suddenly got serious. He shoved his cash back in his pocket. "Not on your life, they're not gonna reopen." The wagon slowed further and began to crawl into position in front of an alleyway near the Hot Spot. Pete nodded his head toward the front cab of the wagon, where Chief Lonnie King sat next to the driver. "Chief's got it out for 'em. *'Don't go soft on 'em,'* he said. Remember? He don't say that for income he cares about. These ones are closing *for good.*"

Thomas fought the rising bile in his throat.

The wagon stopped and the officers got quiet. Through the small windows in the back of the wagon, Thomas saw that the streets were empty. No one lingered in any doorways, and at least for the moment, the sidewalks were clear.

After a moment, the chief opened the back doors of the wagon. His puffy face grinned at the officers as they disembarked. Thomas secured the strap of his helmet under his chin and put a hand to the gun on his hip.

The team gathered outside the van. As they waited for the chief's orders, they milled about, smoking cigarettes, strapping their helmets down, chatting mildly. Thomas was sure he was going to be sick. He glimpsed the chief's face as the officers lined up, ready to raid. The grin he had was ugly and spiteful. In a flash of insight that offered more questions than it answered, Thomas understood that there was a specific reason the chief chose this particular bar—the Hot Spot—to go hard on.

A motive, Thomas heard Molly Malone say in his head.

"Ready, girls?" the chief barked with a menacing grin. Most of the gathered officers affirmed in some way or another. "In we go!"

CHAPTER
TEN

At 11:26 p.m., Molly parked her town car in a dark alleyway across the street from the Hot Spot on Folsom. Though she'd never been to this club before, she knew of it. When Paula mentioned it the other night at Whiskers, Molly could picture the entrance. An old girlfriend had pointed it out once when they'd driven by years ago. Now, seeing the address on the list she'd copied from Lonnie King's office, she understood what the list was—a list of the gay bars they'd intended to shutter.

516 N. Green St. was Whiskers.

529 Folsom St. was the Hot Spot.

That was enough for her. Now to talk to Walter.

The Hot Spot entrance, like so many others, was nondescript and unmarked: a bland door that attempted to disappear into its surroundings. Even so, Molly was sure she'd remember it.

She'd parked close enough for a quick walk to the door,

but far enough away that, to a casual observer, she could appear to be headed in any direction. As Molly slowly strolled closer to the Hot Spot, she realized something was off. The people walking along the street had an air of unease and nervous excitement. Molly soon saw why.

All along the front of the building that housed the Hot Spot, dozens of likely patrons stood with their backs to the wall. They all had grim faces. A few looked badly beaten up. In front of them stood a handful of police officers who periodically pointed a flashlight in someone's face or pushed someone back toward the wall. For the most part, the officers' faces held soft smiles.

A raid, still in progress, but the initial shock of energy seemed to be petering out.

After the briefest of moments to take in the scene before her, Molly quickly retreated into the shadows of an awning that hung over the front door of a bodega.

She didn't recognize any of the patrons lined up along the wall, nor any of the police officers for that matter. As she watched, an officer opened the back of the paddy wagon and began leading the Hot Spot's patrons inside, one at a time.

Suddenly, a muffled blast came from inside the building. Molly instantly knew a gun had been fired. The sound echoed out into the streets where everyone who had gathered outside—passersby, bar patrons, and police officers alike—gave a start.

Molly remembered what Paula said about Walter Newton, owner of the Hot Spot. *He fears he's being followed. I told him to start carrying protection.*

Below her coat, Molly touched her own gun, snuggled alongside her ribcage. Had Walter ended up getting a gun after all? And if he did, had he just used it? Molly wasn't even sure what Walter looked like. Perhaps he was one of the people being loaded into the wagon.

But there was no flurry of gunfire following the shot, no shouts or other noise came from the bar, no one came running out in a panic. The officers in front looked blankly at each other but made no reaction. Perhaps it had been a car backfiring nearby, and because Molly had seen the raid, she'd simply assumed the worst. But the officers she watched simply shrugged and resumed loading people into the wagon.

Molly pulled back into the shadows of the bodega entryway again as she debated her next move. On one hand, going into the Hot Spot now was clearly no longer an option. Even if Walter hadn't been loaded into a wagon during the raid, there was no telling if he'd be alone, away from police officers, where Molly could talk to him. On the other hand, if her suspicions were right, Councilman Carl Owens was behind the raid.

After a moment, Molly's attention was caught by a figure moving slowly toward her on the sidewalk. She was clad in a black evening dress, black gloves, and a black hat too large to ignore. Sylvia Owens.

For a moment, Molly couldn't help but grin softly as she watched Sylvia approach. Her heart began to speed up for a brief moment, watching Sylvia's profile—the shape of her, her gestures and movements. She hadn't appeared to see Molly yet. Instead, her eyes were trained across the street at the slowly diminishing scene in front of the Hot Spot. Molly followed Sylvia's gaze and realized that she wasn't looking in mere casual interest like the few other bystanders were. Sylvia was looking for someone. Someone in the lineup.

Molly's heart beat an even more rapid staccato. *Does she know what this place is?* Molly wondered. She felt a sudden and visceral thrill in imagining that Sylvia not only knew what the Hot Spot was but also had been there before. *Why else would she be here?*

Sylvia took a few steps again, closer to Molly. She appeared to be waiting for a break in the traffic to cross the street.

Molly stepped out of the shadows, slipping herself among the few pedestrians who were making their way along the sidewalk. She casually approached where Sylvia was standing, still looking back and forth across the busy street.

"The crosswalk is much safer, you know," Molly said.

Sylvia's eyes snapped to Molly's. She stared in silence for a moment and then blinked.

"You!" she finally said.

"You too," Molly said with a shrug and a soft smile.

"What are you doing here?" Sylvia lowered her voice, glancing quickly across the street toward the bar. "Where's the detective?" Sylvia retained the slightly frantic energy and movements she'd had the other day.

"Let's go somewhere we can talk," Molly said.

"Oh! I...I can't. Not just now, please. I'm...meeting someone."

"Not here, you're not," Molly said. "Come on. Let's get away from all this." She nodded at the scene across the street.

Molly led Sylvia toward her parked car, hidden in the alley behind the bodega. As they walked, Sylvia gave voice to the many questions that came bubbling up. "I don't understand. Have you come looking for me? How did you know where I'd be? I was going to call this morning, but I couldn't—something came up. Is the detective going to take my case? Did he send you along to find me?"

Molly opened the passenger door of her car for Sylvia and then climbed into the driver's seat.

"Mrs. Owens—" Molly began.

"It's Sylvia. Please."

"The detective didn't send me."

Sylvia pulled back, looking at Molly frankly. "I don't understand."

Molly met Sylvia's gaze and willed herself to not get swept up. "I'm going to level with you, but I need you to do the same in return. I've come to check out the Hot Spot because it's connected to my investigations about your husband's activities."

As Molly spoke, Sylvia's facial expressions fluttered from fear to confusion to something else entirely. Something unreadable.

"*Your* investigations?" Sylvia said. "I don't understand."

When Molly didn't answer immediately, Sylvia asked again, "*Where* is the detective?"

"I'm the detective, Sylvia," Molly said. "Molly

Malone. It's my company. I take steps to make sure it doesn't appear that way, for reasons I'm sure you can imagine."

"Then who…"

"My friend, James, helps me out sometimes. When I need a male face for people to talk to."

Sylvia looked at Molly, taking in this information. "I see."

After a moment, Sylvia's posture softened, but her frown remained. "But isn't it terribly dangerous? For a woman to do this kind of work?" Sylvia moved an inch closer to Molly. Sweet lilacs filled Molly's senses.

She turned her head away from Sylvia's concerned face and unrolled her window a crack. Molly shrugged. "I try not to do stupid things."

"But why were you at the Hot Spot? And what just happened there? I came because…" Sylvia trailed off. "Do you know…what this place is?"

"I know what it is," Molly said. She kept her gaze trained out the window in front of her. She couldn't risk eye contact with the beautiful woman in her car, not right now. Not while they were mutually acknowledging what the Hot Spot was, and what it meant to know what it was. And certainly not while Molly was in the middle of working on her case.

"Last night at the policeman's banquet, I learned some information about your husband. It's caused me to become…curious about his character."

"You heard about his plans? For the city? For people who…" Sylvia's eyes filled with tears. "He's so hateful!

And a hateful man in power—it's just not right. He can't be allowed to…hurt people like that."

Sylvia inched even closer to Molly, until their shoulders could have easily brushed against one another in a way they could both pretend was accidental.

Despite the enticing smell of powder and lilacs coming off Sylvia, Molly remained composed and focused. "Is your husband really trying to kill you? Tell me the truth. All of it."

For a moment, Sylvia didn't respond. She finally took a breath and said, "He *is* killing me. All the time. Every day for the past two years."

"What happened two years ago?"

Sylvia's breath slowed and she sat upright, settling back into the passenger side of Molly's car. Molly breathed slightly easier now. The closeness of Sylvia had begun to be overwhelming.

"I had a friend. A close friend. Someone he didn't approve of. But she was everything to me!" Sylvia buried her face in her hands, her diamond ring glittering in the moonlight. "Please don't hate me. I couldn't bear that."

Molly pulled a handkerchief from her purse and handed it to Sylvia. "I don't quite understand you, Sylvia. But I don't hate you. Certainly not that. I can see you're in pain."

"It's all my fault—his big plan for crushing people he doesn't approve of. People he calls…sexual deviants. *People like me.*" Sylvia looked directly at Molly. The moonlight cast a pearly glow over Sylvia's face. When Sylvia saw that Molly hadn't so much as flinched, she went on.

"He found out about Jane and me. But it wasn't enough to punish *us*. He has to take it out on all of San Francisco. All on account of me."

"I see," was all Molly could say. She flashed on the memory of the lingering look they'd shared in the office.

"I can understand if you'd rather not help me." Sylvia said. "If it makes you uncomfortable." Her voice took on a sober tone. "But please, consider what it means. When it was just me he was upset with, I could bear it. But he's a dangerous man, Molly. He's capable of horrific things. *Please*."

"I'll help you," Molly said. "Because it's personal for me too. Those are my *friends'* places he wants to shut down. My places too." Her cheeks were hot.

Sylvia's eyes widened. "Oh!"

It was rare for this kind of admission to come outside the walls of a place like Whiskers. Those briefly lingering looks shared between queer people were often the only clue Molly could go on—the handsome young clerk at the grocery store with the blond mustache, the woman who worked at Molly's bank, the fellow across the street from Molly's apartment. These people Molly knew as gay outside of the bars only because they'd shared knowing looks and small comments over the years. But with Sylvia Owens—the striking beauty who made Molly's knees weak despite her inner protestations—their shared knowing had come together quite quickly.

Molly broke the moment, pulling away from Sylvia's eyes and gathering her thoughts. "Did someone really try to hurt you? The break-in at your house? The threats? All of that?"

Sylvia's bottom lip quivered. "Yes. Only it didn't happen exactly like I said. It wasn't a stranger. It was my friend's—it was *Jane's* husband. He showed up at the house and threatened me. The horrible things he said! I was so frightened. He didn't attack me, not physically. But telling that story…it was the only way I thought anyone would listen to me. He's a frightening man, Molly. And dangerous."

Molly watched Sylvia's face as she divulged this. There was still something she was holding back. But Molly didn't know where to dig for it. Not yet. And just because Sylvia was also gay didn't mean Molly should automatically trust her. After all, if Molly knew one thing about women, it's that not every attractive lesbian could be trusted.

"What were you looking for tonight?" Molly asked. "You were meeting someone at the Hot Spot?"

Sylvia took a breath, her eyes filling with tears again. "Saturday night while Carl was at the banquet, I stayed home. He'd initially wanted me to come. He told me weeks ago that he'd make sure I was there, knowing how painful it would be to hear him make his announcement. But by Saturday, he must have changed his mind, thank God. While he was out, I searched his office."

"What were you looking for?"

In the moonlight, Sylvia shook her head. "I didn't know for sure. Anything that I could take as evidence to the detective—" Sylvia smiled briefly. "To *you*, I suppose—

that would prove what I told you. He's been working on this speech. He won't let me see it. But I'm sure it's connected. I didn't find the speech. Sometimes he carries it around with him. But I did find letters. From Jane."

"Your girlfriend?"

"Ex-girlfriend," Sylvia replied. "But yes. We'd called it off several weeks before Carl found out about us. We weren't even…doing anything. Just sitting and talking. Figuring out if we could remain friends through it all. But Carl must have guessed what had gone on previously between us. He'd seen the signs."

With a strength she didn't know she had, Molly ignored the impulse to imagine Sylvia in bed with a woman. Molly refocused the conversation. "What did the letters say?"

Sylvia opened her purse and handed some cream-colored pages to Molly. "Read them. There are three."

Molly inspected each letter while Sylvia continued. "I hadn't known she'd written two years ago, let alone so recently," Sylvia started. "And what a relief to get that last letter in time! I read all three letters over and over all night. This morning I even drove through her neighborhood, on the chance that I'd see her. But I was too frightened to drive too close, in case her husband was around. Still, I sat with my car parked near her place for most of the day. I knew it was a long shot to get a chance to see her, but I had to try." As she spoke, Sylvia's gaze bounced around the car, to Molly's eyes, to her hands in her lap, the dashboard, out the window.

"That's why you didn't call."

"Right. I'm sorry about that. I hope it wasn't too much trouble. But I knew if I could just speak with Jane, we could figure something out together and maybe I wouldn't need a detective after all."

"Where did you say you found the letters?" Molly asked. Between the moon, streetlights, and neon signs, she had plenty of light to see them clearly.

"They were in Carl's desk in his office at home."

"How hard to find were they?"

Sylvia shrugged. "Not very. Anyway, I finally left Jane's neighborhood, knowing I would meet her here tonight anyway. But when I arrived and saw the police, I knew it was a raid. I just hope she got away before they showed up. Or perhaps she hasn't even arrived yet... Oh! Do you think Jane's been arrested?" Sylvia's eyes glistened.

"I don't."

"But how can you know?"

"Jane didn't write that last letter," Molly said simply. "And I can't be sure, but I doubt that she was at the Hot Spot tonight, or that she had plans to be."

"I don't understand."

"If what you're saying is true—that it's a goal of Carl's to cause personal anguish to you by destroying places like the Hot Spot—he would have made sure you were at the banquet that night to witness people celebrating this plan of his..."

Sylvia frowned, considering Molly's words. "Go on."

"He'd want to have you on his arm as the picture of all-American values. But you *didn't* attend the banquet and so you were home alone. This gives you the opportunity to happen upon letters he has hidden." Molly paused there, waiting to see how Sylvia took this in.

Outside the car, the street in front of their alleyway had taken on the more typical bustle of a late-night evening in the city. As they spoke, some of the officers had meandered across the street, near the bodega where Molly had taken shelter earlier.

One officer raised a goodbye wave to the driver of the paddy wagon as it departed for the city jail, where the patrons of the Hot Spot—as well as Walter Newton, if he was among them—would be booked for the night, unless they could cough up the bail money, which would be set exorbitantly high to ensure they stayed the night in a jail cell.

Molly's anger flared at the thought.

She turned her attention back to Sylvia. "What I'm asking is—what are the chances he wanted you to find these letters, hoping you'd try to see Jane tonight? So that you would also be here during a planned raid?"

For a moment, Sylvia was silent. She dried the rest of her tears with the handkerchief Molly had given her. She took a few slow breaths and then spoke calmly. "It's strange now that I think of it," she began. "One night, months ago, I'd locked myself in my room when he'd wanted us to go out. I thought for sure he'd break the door down by the way he was pounding on it. Then after a while, it got quiet. Until I heard a noise from outside the balcony doors of my room. He'd climbed up the rose trellis to come through my balcony on the second floor!" Sylvia shook her head. "You may be right. If he'd really wanted me to go to that banquet, he would have found a way to drag me out. Now that I think about it, he didn't put up much of a fight."

Molly nodded. "In this last letter, Jane asks you to meet with her only a few days later, after nearly two years since you two have spoken."

"Right…"

"That happens to be the night the Hot Spot is raided. Unfortunate timing."

Sylvia's mouth dropped open and she looked at Molly, alarmed. "Of course."

"But the most obvious reason," Molly went on, "is that the third letter was *not* written by the same hand as the first two. The penmanship is very close, but the slant is wrong and the *S*'s are off." Molly pointed out the discrepancies between the letters as Sylvia looked closely. "Further, in the first two, she addresses you as *Mrs. Owens* and refers to herself as *Mrs. King*."

"I always hated that," Sylvia said. She'd begun to look through the windshield, watching a trickle of pedestrian traffic meander across the alleyway in front of them. For the second time this evening, she appeared to be looking for someone.

Molly continued. "But in this last letter it's *Sylvia* and *Jane*. Rather abrupt switch to make, especially after two years without contact." She held the letters up again, but Sylvia had stopped looking at them or at Molly.

"Right." Sylvia nodded. Her voice was harder now.

"That means he must be here, then," she said with growing concern.

Molly frowned. "Carl?"

Sylvia shook her head in the negative. Then her eyes finally fixed on something out the windshield of Molly's car. She looked to where Sylvia was pointing.

Standing at the corner of Folsom and the alley where Molly and Sylvia were hidden was a small group of officers. By now, it seemed the raid had finally petered out. At this point, Molly knew it would just be a matter of bolting the doors and writing up the grueling paperwork.

At the center of the group stood Chief Lonnie King, who appeared to be giving some last-minute orders to the officers. His uniform was crisply pressed and his police hat dangled from one hand.

"I just know he's done something dreadful to her," Sylvia said with a thick voice. She sat calmly, but with the faraway look of mourning.

Molly gave a low whistle and steeled herself against the implications of what Sylvia had just revealed. "Just to make sure I have this right," she started, "San Francisco's *chief of police* is your girlfriend Jane's *husband*?"

"Ex-girlfriend," Sylvia replied. "But yes."

"And that's why you couldn't go to the police," Molly said, mostly to herself.

"Yes." Sylvia lit a cigarette.

Molly and Sylvia watched Chief King. He spoke calmly with the few remaining officers. If anyone were to glance down the alleyway, Molly's car would have looked just as dark and lifeless as the rest of the parked cars along the streets and alleys. But the bright lights of the city night didn't offer much cover from closer scrutiny.

Molly pondered for a moment. There was more to this puzzle than she'd thought. Though she had never worked with Lonnie King, his reputation as a crass ogre was well-known. After a moment, Lonnie and the other officers wandered out of sight. "You say you think the chief has done something to Jane? To his own wife?"

Sylvia clamped her eyes shut but tears streamed through anyway. "I knew it was too good to be true. That I might see her again, even as friends. After they first found out about us, Carl was bent on revenge. Lonnie too. There was a murderous rage in both of them. I'd always feared that Lonnie might have killed Jane shortly after he found out. Carl had even insinuated as much. Then, when Lonnie came the house last week and threatened me, he said I'd get what was coming to me, just like Jane had. He talked about her like she was dead." Sylvia held a cigarette in one hand while the other clutched the hand-kerchief to her throat. New tears rolled fatly down her cheeks. "When I found the letters, I thought perhaps I'd been mistaken. That perhaps...Jane was alive after all. Maybe a small part of me realized something was off about the last letter. But I didn't want to take the chance of missing her. I see now that she may indeed have been dead all the while."

After a moment, Sylvia's tears stopped. She looked through the windshield, as though seeing nothing. When she brought her gaze back to Molly she said, "Not only does Carl have the chief of police in his pocket, but Lonnie has it out for me of his own accord. Do you see now how I truly have nowhere else to turn?"

"There's the motive then," Molly said. "I'll help you, Sylvia. No charge. This one's on the house."

"Oh," Sylvia said softly. Then she gave a brief nod. "Thank you."

For a few moments more, they sat in the relative quiet of Molly's car. Molly rolled down her window a few more inches and felt the welcome breeze of the evening. She understood now what she needed to do. It was just a matter of the nuance of how to do it.

On one hand, she was dealing with two prominent people with high-visibility jobs: a city councilman and the chief of police. Which meant gathering evidence could be tricky.

This wouldn't be a typical job where she could easily trail an Average Joe while keeping herself anonymous. On the other hand, she'd already found a way in and out of the police station, and since Sylvia had access to Carl at home, Molly would have a chance to get closer to a subject than usual.

Suddenly, Molly knew what the next move was. It always came—that inner knowing of what's needed next, if only she could quiet her mind long enough to get the message. It would be risky, but it could work.

She quickly explained her plan to Sylvia, covering the key details. When she'd finished, Sylvia nodded, while searching Molly's eyes in a way that felt overly familiar, yet thrilling all the same.

"I can't tell you how much your help means to me." Sylvia rested a hand on the door handle, aiming to exit.

"Of course." Molly was thankful for the relative darkness of the car. She felt her cheeks suddenly grow hot again. Sylvia reached for her hand.

"I don't know what I would do without you…without your help." Sylvia gripped Molly's hand in a tight squeeze, then suddenly leaned forward to pull Molly into a hug.

Molly returned the affection as gingerly as she dared. She let Sylvia's scent envelop her. Her heart beat wildly, wrapped in Sylvia's arms. Though several women had come and gone through Molly's life over the years—had embraced her in this very car, in fact—she'd never felt as electric as she felt with Sylvia, even after knowing her for such a short time. Was it only the thrill of the situation they were in that was drawing them closer? Their hands were still clasped awkwardly between them with one arm flung around each other. Molly wanted to stay in this comfortably uncomfortable hug as long as possible. But she knew they'd already lingered longer than they should.

As she pulled out of the embrace, Sylvia placed a deliberate kiss on Molly's cheek ever so softly, too near her lips to be a mistake. Too much filled with meaning to be a simple kind gesture between new friends. With a brief promise to call Molly at the office in the morning, Sylvia exited the car and slipped away through the neon-lit alleys.

Sylvia's scent lingered. Molly touched her check where she'd kissed her, feeling fluttering in her belly, her throat.

She ran her fingers through her hair to bring her mind back from the imagined pictures that had begun to crystalize in her head.

After a moment, she pointed her sleek black Mercury toward the exit of the alleyway. Before pulling out of the alley onto Folsom, she looked once more at the entrance to the Hot Spot. No pedestrians milled about at this moment. Only two officers remained on site, including Chief King.

Then with a start, she saw Detective Thomas Parker running out the back door of the Hot Spot—sprinting—in the opposite direction of the other officers. He saw a break in the traffic and ran across the street to where Molly's car was poised to join the flow of cars. Officer King yelled something in Thomas's direction, but Molly couldn't catch it over the sound of the traffic. Thomas ran right past Molly's car without seeing her.

His face was red, streaked with tears and marked with a look of shock or despair. Molly watched him run down the block until he was out of sight. She tried to imagine what it was like for him—a police officer who had to conduct arrests of his own friends and community members. It's no wonder he looked such a mess. It was a shame, but their friendship couldn't have survived him doing this kind of work anyway.

Merging into traffic, Molly headed back to her apartment. She'd have to find another way to talk to Walter Newton. She could get his phone number from Paula. If he'd been arrested, he would be hard to get ahold of for the next twenty-four hours at least. In any case, there were other aspects of the case to consider. Lonnie King, for example, and the whereabouts of his wife, if she was even alive.

Of course, the revealing encounter with Sylvia was a thrilling, pulsing experience of its own. Had that goodbye kiss been intentionally close to her mouth? Had it been nothing but an emotionally charged impulse of intimacy? Was she simply an affectionate person? The questions were ceaseless and maddening.

As Molly drove through the summer night, she ran over the details of her plan to ensure there was nothing she'd missed. She couldn't risk a forgotten detail or a deadly misstep.

CHAPTER
ELEVEN

A few days later, Molly and James waited in the detective agency office. When Molly briefed James on what she'd learned from Sylvia, as well as what they'd seen at the Hot Spot, James felt a pressing in his temples. It was all getting to be too much.

But he knew he was in too deep to back out now. Molly couldn't run the rest of this case without him. The plan as Molly described it made sense, though James had been dubious.

"What makes you think he'll take the bait?" James had asked over the phone the night before.

"Carl can't risk it," Molly assured him. "There's too much at stake for him if he gets caught. He'll need to follow any possible whisper of a leak. We just need him in the office so we can record what he says. He won't be able to keep his story straight. *I promise*, James. It'll work."

So now James sat in the office, waiting for Carl to arrive at any moment. As Molly prepped the recording machine below the desk, James opened the *San Francisco Gazette* he'd brought from home.

"Remember to watch the lights," Molly said as she wound up the excess cord from the microphone and tucked it behind the reel-to-reel tape-recording machine under the desk.

"Of course," James said. "This is your show, I know that." He flipped slowly through the newspaper.

Molly rose from the floor and looked at James, her eyebrows raised. "I don't mean to make you feel bad. I just mean you don't have to worry about trying to think up what to do or say. I've figured it all out already, so there's no need to worry. Just keep an eye on the signals and I'll keep you on track."

James nodded, turning back to his newspaper. Suddenly, his breath caught in his throat. He pulled the newspaper closer to his eyes.

Search for Pacific Heights Restauranteur Ends with Grisly Discovery—Eugene Carmine, 54, owner of Gino's Restaurant and Bar at 2504 Fillmore Street in Pacific Heights, was found dead Tuesday morning after a three-week search for his whereabouts. Carmine's body was discovered washed up on Golden Gate Beach by a local fisherman who reported his findings to police. A spokesman for the San Francisco Police Department reported Carmine's cause of death unknown. At this time police have no known witnesses or suspects. No foul play is suspected...

"Oh," said James softly.

Molly peered at the article. "What is it?"

"It's Gene," James said, reading the words over and over. "They found his…they found him."

"Gene who?"

James's throat gripped a painful lump of emotion. He put his face in his hands. "What am I going to tell Lewis?"

He choked back tears. Gene's disappearance had worried him terribly, but of course he couldn't tell Lewis that. He'd needed to be strong. But all the while he'd known something was off. Now, he saw his fears were confirmed. *I need to talk to Lew.*

James felt Molly's arm around his shoulders. She peered over to the article and scanned it.

"A friend of yours? Oh, James, I'm so sorry." Molly hugged him tighter and for once, James allowed himself to be comforted. *Gene, dead? Found washed up on the beach? What kind of world was this?*

Quietly, Molly spoke again. "James?" Her voice came out thick and low. She spoke slowly. "I am *very sorry* to have to tell you this. Especially right now. But I think…I'm almost positive that…that Carl and Lonnie did this."

James whipped his head around, his eyes glistening with tears. *"What?"* He pushed back from Molly's hug.

"The information I found in Chief King's office? I think it was a list of gay bars. That address on Filmore Street—2504—it was on the list. And…it was crossed off."

"Crossed off?" A hot flare of rage filled James's gut, burning out the despair that hadn't yet had time to settle in.

Molly slowly nodded. "Like how you'd cross something off a list when you'd completed it."

Just then the handle of the front office door jiggled as someone tried to enter. The door was locked up tight, but it rattled with the effort and the caller began pounding on the door. "Hello! Open up at once!" James recognized the voice instantly from the podium at the policeman's banquet. It was Carl Owens. His thin voice rang through the frosted glass of the front door.

Molly and James locked eyes.

"Carl," Molly said.

James stood quickly and lunged toward the front door, but Molly stepped in front of him.

"No!" she hissed. "We can't blow this. It has to go exactly as we discussed!" She pushed with all her might against James's chest as he leaned forward.

James softened, then slammed open the bottom drawer of the desk and guzzled two mouthfuls of whiskey from the bottle. He wiped his mouth with the back of his hand, then dabbed at his eyes with his pocket square and blew his nose.

Carl continued pounding on the door, and the glass pane rattled dangerously in its frame. "Hello! I demand to speak to the detective! Open this door!"

"Alright," James said quietly to Molly. He took a deep breath and smoothed his beard with both hands. "I know." He sat down behind the desk and sat up straight. "Let him in."

"You're alright to get through this?" Molly asked. She rested her hands on the desk and leaned forward, holding James's gaze. "James, I need you. Now more than ever." She pointed to the front door, where Carl continued rapping. "We just get him to talk, get it on record, and take it to the mayor. We can't scare him off. Do you understand? We can't let him run. We need to hear it in his own words."

James nodded. "I understand," he said softly. But he wanted to rage and scream and tear the man apart as soon as he walked through the door. His heart pounded in his ears and the lump in his throat was excruciating. "Let him in, Molly."

With trepidation, Molly eased herself back to the front office and closed the door that separated the two rooms.

From his seat at the desk, James heard Carl through his closed office door. "What's the meaning of this?"

He couldn't quite hear Molly's response, but he could make out her surprised and confused tone in whatever she said to Carl. He only had a few brief moments before Molly would let Carl into the inner office.

She was right, of course. This was the moment they had to work with: Carl in the office, a tape recorder underneath the desk. This would be the hardest role he's ever played. James's chest was tight with a grief he couldn't show. His eyes kept catching on certain words on the newspaper in front of him: *found dead...Carmine's body... cause of death unknown.* He took a few slow breaths, vowing to do whatever it took to bring justice to Gene's killers.

Then, Molly's voice came through louder as though she was now standing just outside the inner door. "I quite understand your concern, Mr....?"

"Owens. Carl Owens," came the nasally voice. "Is the detective in? I demand to speak with him at once!"

"Without an appointment, I can't guarantee that he'll see you," Molly said. "But I will check with him to see if he has a spare moment. Wait here, please."

Molly returned to the back office and closed the door behind her. She handed a wrinkled letter to James. He scanned it briefly, seeing that the contents matched what Molly told him about earlier.

"Ready?" she asked in a low voice. James nodded. Molly saw the newspaper still splayed out in front of him on the desk. "Want me to take that?"

"No," James said calmly. "Let him in." He looked at Molly and nodded. "I'm alright. Let him in."

When Carl came through, James stood to shake his hand. At six feet, three inches, James towered above Carl. Carl's hand was damp, as was his face and hairline. His shirt collar looked uncomfortably tight, and his cheeks were red.

James gripped Carl's hand firmly before resuming his seat behind the desk. Carl remained standing, his body rigid as he said, "I demand to know what's going on. This is preposterous."

James reviewed the letter again, making a show of his look of concern and confusion. Finally he spoke. "This is quite remarkable, Mr. Owens—"

"I'll say it is!" Carl jumped in.

"But not only for what this letter insinuates. You see…" James opened his top desk drawer and retrieved a folded piece of paper. "I received a similar letter just this morning." James handed the second letter to Carl. "And look.

See the curl of the penmanship? I do believe they were written by the same hand."

James sat still as he waited for Carl's response. Above the doorframe, Molly's green light lit up.

"The same person?" Carl asked. A look of confusion replaced the bluster he'd barged in with.

"It must be," James said. "But to what end? My letter says that a man with the initials C.O. would be paying me a visit—I know now that must be you, sir—and that it would be in both our best interests to work together to deliver a sum of money to this post office box." James held up the two letters side by side. Falling into the role of detective helped him swallow his rage. He wanted more than ever to continue making Carl squirm. "Your letter instructs you come to *my* detective agency and says that I would be your *best option* to avoid being exposed for…what was it?" James pulled Carl's letter closer to his face for a better look. "Ah yes, for your *'murderous plot.'* I'll have to be honest with you, Mr. Owens, I know less about this than you do. What is this referring to? What have you gotten wrapped up in?"

"I—" Carl's eyes darted as he avoided James's direct gaze. "I haven't any—"

James looked away and pulled out a notebook, taking his time to find and sharpen a stubby pencil. He calmly organized the items on his desk, giving Carl time to figure out his story. After a few moments, Carl spoke up. "It must be because of the new initiative I've started. Some deranged citizen who knows what I'm worth and is seeking to blackmail me."

James began taking notes. "Initiative? Tell me about that."

"I'm surprised you haven't heard of it." Carl finally took a seat across the desk from James. His eyes gleamed as he talked about his plan. "As a city councilman, I am single-handedly closing every sick and dirty gathering place for the lowest of the low in this city."

"Single-handedly?"

"Completely." Carl nodded. Then, seeing James's confused frown, said, "Well, I mean…with the help of the police force, of course."

"Of course." James sipped from his coffee mug, then took a beat before moving on. "Who is this other fellow mentioned in the letter? *'Officer L.K.,'* it says." James frowned. "A police officer. Where do I know those initials…?" James pretended to think.

"I'm sure I don't know. It could be any—"

"Lonnie King! That's it!" James adopted a bright look on his face. "The San Francisco chief of police—our esteemed Chief King. Are you in business with him?

"Business? Well, no. I *know* him, of course. He's a…"

"A friend?" James offered when Carl trailed off.

Carl quickly shook his head. "Not that. We are professional colleagues. We share similar views and politics."

"Your letter warns you, *'Do not approach Officer L.K. about this letter or your entire agreement will fall through.'* Tell me, Mr. Owens, what agreement is that?"

Carl's eyes darted around the room once more. Behind Carl, the green light lit up again. James sat back in his chair and glanced down at the recorder to see that the reels were spinning as they should. They were.

"I'll tell you one thing, Mr. Owens," James started when Carl still hadn't spoken. "I can appreciate a confidential agreement between gentlemen. I'm not asking out of personal interest in the matter. Your business is your business, of course. But if you want my help—and I'll assume your being here means that you do—then I'll need to know the whole picture of what we're dealing with. I'll ask again. What is this *murderous plot*? You have to understand I can only help you if I know what the situation is."

"I'll tell you," Carl finally said. "Lonnie had the idea that in the process of the *legal* closing of these places of ill repute, if one or two individuals happened to get…to get *caught in the crossfire*, well, that's just too bad for them for being somewhere they shouldn't be in the first place."

"I see. A sort of *wrong place at the wrong time* situation." James let out a hard, sardonic laugh. "And this was the police chief's idea?"

Carl nodded firmly. "Indeed, it was."

"Tell me about the agreement. Where do you come into play in all this?"

Carl rubbed the back of his neck. "As the political arm of the initiative, my part in this is…to clear the red tape that would ensnare the officers from doing their jobs properly."

"In other words, to look the other way."

"Certainly not," Carl objected. "Everything we are doing is well within the law, I can assure you. How the chief of police chooses to direct his police force is out of my control. I'm only involved on the policy and legal side of things, you see."

James nodded. "Should I assume there is a financial arrangement between the two of you?"

Carl said nothing. James continued. "Let's imagine there is. Is there anyone else who could know about such an arrangement?"

The red light above the door flashed. Instantly, James regretted the question, realizing that Carl would immediately think of Sylvia. He needed to pivot quickly.

"There's no arrangement, I can assure you of that," Carl said. "But *you're* the detective here, not me. As far as I know *you* could be the one who's behind all this. You received a letter as well. Why are you, among all the detectives in the city, being brought in by this—this mysterious letter writer?" Carl leaned back in his chair, positioning his fingers in a steeple. He cocked his head and considered James.

"Me?" James said. His anger at Carl was only growing more steadily. The longer he had to sit across a desk from this vile man and pretend to be on his side, the more his anger grew. "But that's preposterous, Mr. Owens. It's just as I've told you. I received a letter myself just this morning. I'm just as in the dark about all this as you are."

Carl considered this. Then, he looked down, past his crossed legs, past his shining shoes, to a spot underneath James's desk. With a start James realized he was looking where Molly had been setting up the recording machine. Had she hidden it well enough? She was in the middle of preparing it when Carl had knocked. But had she finished putting the box and wires and tape reels in position before unlocking the door to let him in?

Slowly, Carl's eyes moved back up to James's face. "Are you recording me?" he said with an eerie calm.

James froze. He had to carefully choose what to say next. He couldn't very well pretend there wasn't a recording device under his desk when Carl was looking right at it. On the other hand, he couldn't tell Carl the whole truth. He was stuck. And before he'd been able to command the authority of the situation, Carl had done it himself.

After a moment, the green light appeared above the door behind Carl.

"Yes, Mr. Owens. I am recording you."

"Why?"

James glanced at the lights again. Both were dark. "It's...customary. In case I need to refer back to what a client has told me in a first meeting." James was rewarded with a green light for his improvisation.

Carl squinted. He looked unsure. "What do you know that you're not telling me? Who hired you?"

"I assure you no one has hired me, Mr. Owens. This letter came to me this morning."

"Hand-delivered?"

"What's that? Well, I don't know..."

"There's no postage on the envelope. Same as mine. Someone *hand-delivered* these letters. Who brought it to you?"

Above the doorframe, both lights remained unlit. *Molly, where are you? I need help!* Carl cocked his head, watching James's face. It was now James's turn to squirm in his chair.

Finally, James said firmly, "My *secretary* brought me the letter this morning. We'll have to ask *her* where it came from." He spoke loud enough that Molly could have heard him even without the bugged room. As much as James hoped Carl didn't pick up on the anger in his voice, he hoped Molly did.

Carl launched out of his chair and opened the door between the back office and the front reception room and barked at Molly, "Who brought this letter?"

James followed quickly behind Carl's heels and watched as Molly swiftly closed the top drawer of her desk, concealing the tiny speaker and switches inside. The armpits of James's shirt were soaked through, and his head was pounding. The summer heat made the air in the office stale. He felt like he couldn't quite take a full breath. His fury at the whole situation was close to boiling over. But for a moment at least, Carl was Molly's problem.

"Answer me, girl!"

Molly's eyes got big as she looked back and forth between the two men. She shook her head, stumbling over her words. "I...I...I don't—I wasn't, I mean..."

"Well, spit it out!" Carl said. Then, turning to James, "Is she stupid?"

"She can be," James answered, his eyes fixed on Molly.

"I just found it!" Molly finally got out. "I was in here, opening up the office, when I heard something. I turned around and...and then I saw it, there on the floor. I guess someone must have...slipped it under the door!"

"Under the door?" Carl looked at the bottom of the door, as though any further clues might remain there.

He began to slowly pace around the office, mumbling softly to himself. He slicked his hair back repeatedly and adjusted his tie and suit jacket absent-mindedly as he thought. James stared at Molly across the office. She said nothing. She only returned his look, shaking her head as though she didn't know how to help.

Finally, Molly spoke up. "Now that I think of it, it may have been a police officer."

James and Carl's eyes both opened wide at this. Molly looked at each of them steadily, then continued. "I opened the door to see if I could catch whoever it was. All I saw was a man walking away at the end of the hall. I can't be sure, but I believe I remember a policeman's uniform."

Carl let out a sharp laugh. He smiled sardonically. "That bastard."

"Is that helpful?" Molly asked.

"Mighty helpful," Carl said. "Thank you, sweetheart." He returned to James's office and gestured for James to follow him. "Detective?"

Back in the office, Carl paced the room.

"Old Lonnie boy is trying to shake me out for more money," he said, mostly to himself. He slowly meandered around the furniture in James's office, working through his idea. "For some reason he's looped you into the deal too. Which is smart, actually. He knows he can't involve someone else from the police force, so he found a *nobody* to drag into the mix." Carl snapped his fingers. "But I'm going to turn that around. Make it work in my favor. He won't see it coming."

As Carl paced, working through his theory, James's eyes rested on the folded newspaper on his desk. The article headline seemed to bellow at him, the words "Grisly Discovery" standing out larger than they had before. James glanced at the clock and wondered if Lewis had gone out for the newspaper yet. *I don't want Lewis finding out without me there. He'll be in so much grief. I have to break the news gently.*

James looked away from the newspaper to find that Carl was pointing at him. "You're coming to my house."

"Me?" James's heart beat quicker.

"That's right. I'll make sure Lonnie pays me a visit tomorrow night. You'll be there, hidden somewhere. With that." He pointed under the desk to the recording machine.

"But what will I say?"

"You leave that to me." Carl said.

Behind Carl's head, the green light lit up. *Dammit, Molly.*

CHAPTER
TWELVE

Once Carl had blustered his way out of the detective's office, Molly closed the door behind him. *Not exactly as I'd planned,* she thought. *But this could be even better. Get them both in one place, record everything, and then turn them in.*

In the back office, James had begun gathering his coat, hat, and briefcase. "I need to get home to Lewis," he said.

Molly nodded, then tentatively asked, "I'll see you tomorrow, then?"

For a moment, James said nothing.

Please, James, I need you. "I'll come with you to Carl's house," Molly promised. "I'll hide somewhere nearby. Sylvia will help set it up, I'm sure of it. I'll be there the whole time and I won't let you down."

"Not like you let me down in there?" James loosened his necktie and rolled up his sleeves. His face was red. The warmth of midday had begun creeping through the windows and the small office was already muggy. He paced the room, angrily gesturing at the drawer that held Molly's switch. "Where were your lights, Molly? Red light, green light. Stop, go. *Speak up, puppet!*"

"I'm sorry. I know, I froze. This is so hard—"

"Bullshit!" James quickly stepped close to Molly. "You don't know what's hard," he said gruffly. Tears filled to the rims of his eyes. "I just had to shake the hand of someone who had my friend killed. Hell, he may have killed Gene himself. And I had to pretend to be *happy* to work with him. I had to sit across a desk from him and *play nice* and act out my little part as though I'm not raging inside. *That's* hard. *Fuck you.*" He pushed past Molly out the door of the detective agency and all but ran down the hallway toward the building's exit onto Ohlone Street.

Fuck.

Forged letters from a presumed dead woman.

A crooked politician and foul-playing police chief.

At least one man almost certainly murdered.

And what of the sound she'd heard at the Hot Spot raid? Perhaps it had been a gunshot after all. The morning after the raid she'd called Paula at home to see if she'd heard anything from Walter, but there was no answer, and then Molly had gotten engrossed in her new strategy. Rapidly, the clues reorganized themselves in her mind. The gunshot sound, Thomas running away with that horrified look on his face. Had Walter been shot while Molly was busy canoodling with Sylvia in an alleyway? And where was Jane King?

What have you gotten yourself into, Malone?

That one of the victims was a friend of James and

Lewis was too much to bear. Her heart ached at the thought of James telling Lewis the awful news about Eugene. It was unbearable. But now she understood definitively what it meant that Gino's Restaurant was crossed off Chief King's list. Molly pulled her notebook from her coat pocket and reviewed the notes she'd copied in King's office. It wasn't just a list of bars they'd planned to close.

It was a hit list.

Molly had only one concern then. *Paula.* She had to warn Paula.

But first, she called Sylvia at home. With Carl only a few moments gone from her agency's front door, she knew Sylvia would be undisturbed at home. As quickly as she could, Molly debriefed Sylvia on how the plan with the letters went.

"So it backfired," Sylvia's voice crackled through the phone line.

"Not at all," Molly insisted. "It didn't go the way I expected, but that doesn't mean it won't work. In fact, this is better. If Carl and Lonnie turn on each other, they can't help but say incriminating things. All of which will be recorded. It will all work out just fine. But we need to be deliberate about a few details. Can you help me?"

Sylvia agreed to help Molly with a second attempt at setting up a sting. Molly gave Sylvia instructions to set up the space, and they arranged a way for Molly to remain hidden throughout the whole interaction.

"Sylvia," Molly said tentatively before hanging up. "Thank you. We couldn't do any of this without you, you know."

Molly locked up the office behind her and made her way swiftly toward Whiskers. As she passed the familiar buildings and storefronts and alleyways, it occurred to her that she'd never made this journey during the brightest part of the day before.

Like anyone else visiting Whiskers on a regular basis, Molly was used to only visiting under cover of darkness, hidden from broad view. And perhaps also hidden by the supposition that at the end of the day, when people are tired, and their bellies are full from their downtown date night dinners and they're feeling a little sleepier, they might not notice the gatherings of people who conceal themselves behind nondescript doors night after night.

Signs in storefront windows caught Molly's attention in ways they hadn't before:

Artichokes for Sale.

Seamstress Available for Hire.

Piano Lessons Here, Cheap.

Here, in the windows she walked past dozens of times, were signs of a life she didn't know existed in her neighborhood. It gave her a quaint feeling of home. Molly felt astonished that even among the chaos of a city—the traffic that grew day by day, the new construction of industry giants that perpetually expanded the city, the bustle of one of the largest American cities in 1943—one could still find pockets of slow living. Pockets of community.

If Whiskers disappeared, where would Molly find community? Where could people like her, like Sylvia, Paula and her cousin Natalia, James, Lewis, and everyone else she knew and loved—where would they all gather to feel seen? To feel safe? To feel connected in the middle of the bustle of a country that wished they would disappear?

Of course, simply losing Whiskers wasn't Molly's biggest concern. If Whiskers got shut down, she'd find another spot to spend time. But if anything happened to Paula…that was just too much. And regardless, if Lonnie and Carl had their way, there would be no other places to for Molly's community to gather anyway.

She had to warn Paula. At least Molly could buy her some time.

Tomorrow she and James would have Carl and Lonnie in one place, where they could record the conversations and even confront them both if needed. Then they would take their evidence to Mayor Booker, who would see to it that Carl and Lonnie were brought to justice.

Molly just hoped tomorrow wouldn't be too late.

CHAPTER
THIRTEEN

As she approached the alleyway that led to Whiskers' main entrance, it occurred to Molly that the door might be locked this early in the day. If it was, she'd have to figure out how to get into the building another way. It wouldn't be the first time in recent days she'd have to break into a familiar building on short notice.

But Molly was in luck. She rounded to corner to find both Paula and Natalia in the alleyway where Whiskers' door was nestled—unmarked, though the rusty numbers hanging from the stucco wall confirmed the address: 516 N. Green Street. Paula and Natalia were unloading wooden crates from a delivery truck that idled partway down the alley.

"Molly Malone, is that you?" Natalia carefully set down a crate before greeting Molly with a hug.

Paula wiped her brow with a bandana she'd produced

from the back pocket of her jeans. "A little early today aren't you, friend?"

"I'm not here for social hour. Though a drink sounds mighty fine at the moment."

Paula took a couple steps closer to Molly, studying her face. "You look spooked. You okay? Want to talk inside?"

"Please." Molly followed Paula inside as Natalia continued unloading crates from the delivery truck and carrying them through to the back rooms of the bar.

Over Paula's heavy pour of whiskey, Molly explained her concerns. She described Lonnie King and Carl Owens's plans, and how she'd already suspected them of being behind the murder of Eugene Carmine of Gino's Restaurant.

"I was outside the raid at the Hot Spot the other night, and I think I heard a gunshot. Paula, I'm sorry to say—I think that—"

"I heard about Walter," Paula said flatly. She downed her shot. After a moment spent looking at the empty cup, she poured another one for herself, then simply held the glass in her hands, gazing at the amber liquid. "A sting gone wrong, I guess. I told him to get some protection for himself."

Paula spoke slowly, her voice choked with emotion. "Maybe he panicked when they showed up. You know how it is—if the cops see a gun, they'll shoot. I should have done a better job of preparing him." She shook her head, then sniffed and wiped her face with both hands and gave a soft shrug. "I couldn't protect him, but I could have helped him protect himself. I appreciate your concern for it all and for coming here to tell me about it. That stuff I told you the other night about people going missing? I feel real bad about all of that. But there's nothing I can do for them."

"I'm not asking you to protect anyone but yourself," Molly said. "I came here just to warn you and…and your *family* about what's going on. You are on their list. I saw it. I think you're next."

Natalia had paused in her trips in and out of the building unloading the truck. She and Paula passed a look between them that Molly couldn't read. Then, Paula nodded at Natalia, who closed the front door of Whiskers before disappearing into the back room, leaving Paula and Molly alone.

Paula smiled gently. Tears glistened in her eyes. "You know who my family is. They don't need protecting." She laid a hand gently on Molly's arm. "And neither do I."

"I'm telling you, Paula. I don't like it. It's different this time. They're breaking more rules than usual."

Paula moved to the other side of the bar to pour them both more whiskey. Molly gestured that she was done drinking. "Why won't you listen to me?"

Just then, Natalia reappeared from the back room. She locked eyes with Paula and said, "He wants to hear what she has to say."

"Who?" Molly asked. She looked back and forth between the two of them.

Natalia looked to Paula for a response.

Eventually Paula shrugged and nodded. Drying her hands on a small bar towel, Paula turned to Molly. "Would you like to meet my Uncle Val? I could say he's requesting to see you, but Uncle Val doesn't make requests." She spoke with a good-natured grin, but Molly understood her to be perfectly serious.

"Your uncle?" Molly looked back and forth between Paula and Natalia.

"He's *Uncle Val* to Paula," Natalia said. "*Papa* to me."

"Valentino Fazio? *The Don?*" Molly asked, her heart beating quickly.

Paula gave a soft laugh, her tears mostly dried up by now. "The very one. He's in the back just now. Visiting us along with this month's delivery." She nodded toward the alleyway, where the delivery truck had been idling full of crates—crates of Fazio family whiskey, Molly now understood.

"You're not in trouble," Natalia said, matching Paula's reassuring grin. "He knows you're in our good graces."

"He knows what kind of work I do?"

Paula and Natalia exchanged looks again. "He knows," Natalia said.

"Oh—and don't call him *the Don*. He hates that," Paula smiled. "He'll insist on *Valentino*. He does for all his friends."

His friends. Is that what Molly was to the notorious Fazio family—a friend? Sure, she considered herself a friend to Paula and Natalia. In truth, she often forgot they were Fazios. In Molly's mind, they were just the operators of her favorite watering hole.

But *Valentino Fazio?* She might as well consider herself friends with Al Capone.

In her head, she heard his name in the same way it was displayed across the front pages of the newspapers—loud and bold and slightly chilling: "Valentino Fazio, Fearsome Don of the American West Fazios," they called him. Seeing him in real life was not something Molly ever thought she'd experience.

She followed Natalia and Paula through the door to the back rooms of Whiskers, somewhere Molly had never ventured in all her evenings at the club. They passed an open doorway to what appeared to be a storage room: there were shelves full of bottles of alcohol, glassware, extra candles, and bar napkins, all neatly organized.

They reached the back office, where Natalia gave a brief courtesy knock before entering. The back room of Whiskers was nothing like Molly had imagined. It wasn't a cold and seedy basement corner with broken furniture and dusty shelves of booze. Instead, it was a cozy environment, set up like a quaint living room with a braided rug, a low coffee table, a clean and comfortable couch and matching armchairs, floor lamps, bookshelves, and a long desk spotlit by a green glass banker's lamp.

When they entered the room, Valentino Fazio was standing in front of a large painting, an oil landscape of greens and oranges and blues. He held a cut crystal highball glass half-full of whiskey. He turned with a gleaming smile, then set his glass down on the coffee table.

He was not a tall man, barely taller than Molly herself. That Natalia Fazio was his daughter made Molly wonder what Natalia's mother looked like. Natalia towered several inches above her notorious father.

Valentino's mostly gray hair was styled neatly but not overly fussily. His suit was crisp without seeming overdone, and his smile was genuine—the same as Molly had seen in the news photographs. Although usually that smile was framed next to some blazing, scandalous headline or another.

"Molly Malone," he said warmly. He took both of her hands in his own, as though he were a knight helping a delicate lady down from a carriage. He kissed the knuckles of both of her hands quickly and finished with a kiss on each cheek.

Molly flushed, thrown off by the exuberant display of affection. *This is the most I've been kissed by a man in a long time,* she thought with bemusement.

Valentino Fazio smelled of spiced cologne. "I hear you know of something that concerns my family." He gestured to a spot on the couch across from him. "Please, sit."

Molly settled into the deeply cushioned couch. "Thank you for speaking with me, Mr. Fazio—"

"Please—call me Valentino."

Behind him, Paula smiled and splayed out her hands palms up in a gesture that said, *And there you have it.*

"I'll just get into it," Molly said. "I'm concerned for Paula's safety. Maybe Natalia's, too. It's hard to say for sure. But before you laugh at me...I know who you are, and if I thought that would be enough, I'd leave it alone. But even knowing about the connections you have, I thought you'd want to know."

Valentino gave her a warm smile. "Sweet child. I do not *have* connections. I *am* the connection. My dear Natalia has told me of your concerns. I asked her to allow me to hear it from you. Now, why you have brought your concerns to my family? Because you know who I am, what is it that you think I cannot handle?" Valentino spoke deliberately, in no rush, with the confidence of someone who knew that whenever he spoke, he spoke to a rapt audience. His gaze remained easy and kind, though something dark simmered behind his eyes that gave Molly a chill.

"I know you have an agreement with law enforcement that lets you run Whiskers without any trouble." Paula, Natalia, Valentino—the Fazios, all—looked at Molly blankly.

"I'd bet there's a lot more to it than that," she continued. "I'm not interested in the details. I don't give a damn what you do with your money. The point is, your money is no good anymore—" Valentino gave a surprised laugh. "The vice squad is about to raid Whiskers. I don't know when. Probably soon. They're going to break your deal— whatever agreement you've had. You managed to survive Atherton's time, but now Carl Owens wants to run the city and the chief is in on it. It's personal for them *both*—Councilman Carl Owens and Chief Lonnie King." Molly looked at Paula, willing her to understand what she meant without spelling the whole thing out. "They are *personally* driven by anger and revenge for reasons I won't go into. The point is, this isn't about morals or political career moves for either of them. They want *revenge*. On our community specifically. And not just that, but I'm afraid… I'm afraid they mean to kill Paula."

"Molly Malone," Valentino said. His easy smile had

disappeared. He spoke frankly but not without kindness. "I have to say I very much appreciate your concern for the Fazio family. This does my heart good to feel loved by you in such a manner. But I would never let anyone hurt the people I love. Paula has nothing to fear, I give you my word on that promise. The dealings my family has with individuals who may or may not hold careers in government or law enforcement sectors—these dealings are not to be trifled with. And anyone who is involved in them knows that. If what you are suggesting were true, then I would indeed be concerned. But not for Paula. For the lives of these men you have named." Valentino picked up his tumbler and took a leisurely drink. Without his smile, Valentino's steady gaze was chilling. Molly understood at once how this man, short though he might be, was able to command so much obedience.

He set the tumbler down again and inched himself forward in his chair. His fingers formed a steeple as he continued speaking. "As anyone I do business with understands, I do not suffer fools gladly, as they say. I am an honest businessman, and my family is everything to me. Anyone who would consider threatening my kin would find themselves in an undesirable circumstance. Anyone I do business with offers life and limb as collateral to work with me. This is why I can assure you these men you have named—Owens and King, is it?—will certainly *not* be taking any mutinous action against my family. For to move against *my family* is to move against me, *Valentino Fazio*. And to do such a thing..." He shook his head and chuckled. "Only one with the wish of death would do such a thing."

Valentino stood up from the armchair, and Molly followed suit. Somehow he seemed much taller than when she'd first seen him.

"Now I ask that you set your mind at ease and be on your way. Come back tonight when Whiskers is open for business and Paula will give you anything you want, on the house." He smiled broadly at Paula, who nodded to indicate she'd be sure to do just that. "In fact—" Valentino picked up a slim brown bottle from one of the wooden crates Natalia had carried in. "Take one on me."

Molly was struck silent by Valentino's kind but firm dismissal of her concerns. She found herself suddenly holding the bottle in her hands. "I'm telling you, they've *killed* people for this," she said, her voice sounding weaker in her insistence. "Whiskers was on their list. I saw it myself!"

"I understand what you think you saw, Molly Malone. I tell you now to leave it alone. It is none of your concern."

Paula and Natalia had begun slowly walking toward the door, indicating to Molly that it was, indeed, time for her to go. Molly draped her jacket over one arm, concealing the bottle beneath it.

"All I'm asking is that you keep your eyes open," she said to Paula. "They don't simply want these places closed, they want us *dead*. They're picking off owners, one by one. No matter what *connections* someone has." She made her last point firmly to Valentino, who had fixed her with a steady gaze.

CHAPTER
FOURTEEN

The following morning, Sylvia Owens awoke early as usual. The deep navy of the night had barely faded in favor of the soft pink sunrise. From her balcony window, Sylvia watched the chilling fog that would eventually give way to another warm summer day. Her home atop a sloping hill in Sea Cliff gave an inspiring view of the mighty Pacific. The impressive reach of the Golden Gate Bridge across the water beckoned Sylvia to escape the confines of life with Carl. She'd told herself that once the bridge was complete, she would find a way to leave. But that was years ago, and here she was, still on the balcony looking at it.

Traffic through her neighborhood streets picked up with early commuters. Shortly, Carl would be among them.

Once the sound of the front door closing echoed upstairs to Sylvia's second floor room, she pulled her silk robe tighter around herself and made her way down the sweeping staircase.

Tonight, Molly Malone would be in her house.

What a lady. There was a fluttering in her belly, a gripping in her thighs. When she'd sought out a private detective the week prior, it was by mere happenstance that she picked the agency she did. Sylvia had known that her visit to the office that Saturday morning might lead to nothing, but Carl unexpectedly left early for some unknown errand that day, so Sylvia had jumped at the chance to visit the agency.

She was relieved when someone answered the door.

Finding out Molly wasn't merely the secretary of the agency as she'd assumed but was in fact the detective was a bit of a shock. But what left her reeling was learning that Molly was also a lesbian. That she knew what the Hot Spot was.

The information was almost too much all at once. But once Molly had explained her reasons for hiding her true identity, Sylvia understood perfectly. *Of course,* she realized after Molly had revealed her secrets, *women have always invented harmless stories to keep the men around them from hurting themselves with their idiotic rages.* Because that's just what Sylvia had done.

Carl's suspicions of Sylvia's misdeeds were always unfounded. Until he drove her to the point where they weren't. And by then, she didn't care anymore. Long before Jane came around, Sylvia understood that Carl's mean-spirited behavior would never change. No matter what she did to make things right with him, he would always insist on having the upper hand. He never wanted an equal partner through life. He wanted someone subservient to him.

Carl had no understanding of how to be a leader. He wanted blindly loyal followers who wouldn't question or challenge him. He wanted the power and prestige that came with being in charge without any of the responsibility, discipline, or compassion that comes with leading, inspiring, or encouraging anyone. He was made to be a dirty politician.

It wasn't until Jane came along that Sylvia experienced the kind of love she felt built for. Reciprocal, compassionate, and above all, based on mutual respect. Sylvia had always known she was more attracted to women than to men, and she'd had schoolgirl dalliances with other women in her younger days. But Jane was the first woman she'd spent significant time with over several collected months.

It was with Jane that Sylvia had begun to imagine what life with another woman could look like. Making meals together, taking trips into the hills to enjoy time in nature, having lunches on sunny patios—going places their husbands would never take them.

The time Sylvia had with Jane appeared to build toward a relationship. Jane King was kind, caring, easy to talk to. Intimacy with Jane was lovely and soft and delicious. But Jane would never leave Lonnie—had no interest in it, in fact. As much as she'd talk about how hard on her he was, she also vehemently refused to consider what life with Sylvia could be. Which is what ultimately tore them apart. Sylvia had seen Lonnie's temper before, so she understood Jane's fear of him. But her refusal to even consider a way out was confounding. Finding a way out of her marriage was all Sylvia thought about.

It was during her time with Jane that Sylvia realized there was more for her in the world than simply being Carl Owens's wife. When they'd first married, Sylvia had been won over by Carl's charisma, a facade he now only pulled out for strangers, colleagues, or anyone else he was trying to impress. After the first few charmed years, he'd dropped the show for Sylvia, who was finally able to see who he truly was.

So by the time she met Jane, Sylvia was desperate to get out. Perhaps she wouldn't be with Jane for the rest of her life. Perhaps she'd be alone. That didn't matter. All that mattered was that she could be free.

Though their romance was short-lived, it was intense and left her with a feeling of promise for her future. Jane seemed content to continue their dalliances in secret, but Sylvia knew she needed more than that. And there was Jane's infuriating insistence on calling her *Mrs. Owens* all the time.

Sylvia never wanted to be *Mrs.* anyone. She wanted to be herself, first and foremost. Not someone's wife. Just someone. Jane was not the love of Sylvia's life, but their time together marked a time of change. At least it did for Sylvia.

"Poor Mrs. King," Sylvia murmured to herself as she switched on the living room radio in its gleaming teak cabinet. Helen Forrest's golden voice crooned in between swelling horns and easy strings:

You are the promised kiss of springtime that
makes the lonely winter seem long...

It was far too romantic of a song for a weekday morning, but the words touched on the budding feelings Sylvia felt in the center of her chest, her belly.

Romantic feelings for Molly, yes. But she recognized that her fascination with Molly was similar to those she had anytime she met another gay or lesbian person: a feeling of recognition and community.

And yet, her interest in Molly wasn't just because she was a lesbian. And it wasn't just that she'd put a strategy in place to stop Carl. Meeting the brown-eyed beauty who was Molly Malone was the last thing Sylvia expected when she finally decided to tell someone about what she knew of Carl's rotten plans. But there was something in Molly that Sylvia recognized as *home*. If she were younger, she might have skipped around the room for how she felt. But the looming vision of what they were going to attempt put the prospect of skipping far from her mind. As much as her defiance of Carl fortified her, she felt terrified about what was at stake, what she could lose.

Crossing through to the kitchen, Sylvia put on the kettle and prepared her coffee. Rich, dark, a generous swirl of cream. She rubbed sleep from her eyes. Carl hadn't bothered to tell her that Lonnie King would be coming by the house later in the evening, though of course she knew he would be, thanks to Molly's call yesterday.

She had been anxious to hear how it went with Carl in Molly's office. Even though Molly explained how her operation worked—where her friend James sat and how they communicated from separate rooms. Still, Sylvia was terribly worried that Carl would find out the truth.

She'd pictured nearly every manner of worst-case scenario for how that meeting could go, especially knowing that Carl would be in a rage when he received the anonymous letter at his office in city hall. But she'd never imagined she'd have to participate in a sting operation in her own home. Molly had assured her everything would work as planned, and perhaps it was foolish, but Sylvia believed her. She was desperate to believe her.

There was no telling what the fallout of tonight's conversation between Lonnie and Carl would be. Maybe it would all go wrong and Molly wouldn't get whatever evidence she needed to stop them. Or maybe Carl would see Molly hiding and try to hurt her.

Still, Molly was a professional. She'd assured Sylvia over the phone that there was nothing to worry about. When Carl had gotten home from the detective agency after finding Molly's forged letter, he'd been seething with a frightening anger toward Lonnie King—a good sign, of course. With Carl focused on taking down Lonnie, perhaps it would all work out after all. At least she could stop the terror they'd already begun.

Since coming clean with everything in Molly Malone's car, Sylvia understood that Jane was probably dead. And if by some chance Jane *was* alive, Sylvia knew she'd likely never hear from her again. In the time since Carl and Lonnie found out about them, she imagined Jane's life couldn't have been any easier than Sylvia's was. In fact, Jane very likely had it much worse. Though Carl and Lonnie were cut from the same cloth, Lonnie's mean streak turned toward physical harm, whereas Carl's was more psychological.

Meeting Molly was the strangest thing. What Sylvia felt for Molly was similar to what she had with Jane, but somehow it was more grounded. That Molly had created a career for herself showed her drive and eagerness to work and be productive. Molly felt comfortable in her own skin. Being a lesbian didn't seem to be something shameful for Molly, as it had been for Jane.

But for now, Sylvia couldn't think about all that. She needed to prepare for this evening. She'd have to see Lonnie King's ugly mug in her own home. She prayed for the strength to keep her emotions in check. To not get stuck in fear, to not clam up, to not let him intimidate her.

In just a few short hours, Molly Malone, the dreamy lady detective with the soothing eyes, an air of confidence and strength, and a smile that Sylvia couldn't look away from, would be in her own home. Her face went hot as she remembered the kiss she had so brazenly planted on Molly's cheek. It was exhilarating.

After she'd made the few arrangements in the house that Molly requested, all she needed to do was wait.

CHAPTER
FIFTEEN

L ater that evening, Molly and James drove through the city toward the Sea Cliff neighborhood. They sat mostly in silence. Molly attempted conversation, but James shut her down each time, at best giving a brief response to whatever topic she initiated.

As Molly maneuvered her car through the curved streets of Sylvia's posh neighborhood, James gazed out the passenger window without any indication of what he might be thinking.

Molly's chest felt tight and her nerves frayed. She'd never before been so affected by her work. But of course, this job was different. It was personal. Not only that, to know that she'd let James down on so many occasions was too much to bear. Worse still, she didn't have a clue as to how to fix it.

When they were a few blocks away from the Owenses' residence, Molly pulled her car to the side of a tree-lined neighborhood street. The sun was just setting. With the car still running, Molly got out and moved to the backseat of the car. She lay down as flat as possible across the bench seat and covered herself with a checkered blanket made of thick wool. James took over driving from there.

Hidden in the back, in the darkness of the blanket, Molly felt even more stupid about the whole thing. James was her dearest friend. He and Lewis were her family— some of the closest people she had in this world. But lately she'd treated James like dirt. She hadn't done it on purpose, of course. She hadn't realized how much she'd been taking advantage of James's good nature. After the Owens case was handled, she would make amends to him. To him and Lewis both. Somehow.

Molly wedged herself in the seat as the car veered to the right. Then the car slowed, perhaps as James looked for street numbers on the houses and mailboxes. Finally, he came to a stop.

"We're here," James said quietly from the front seat. "5809. Blue front door."

Molly peeked out from her blanket and saw they were parked under a large tree on a quiet street of stately homes. The house with the blue door was large and imposing. Two cars were parked in the driveway, one after the other. "Great," Molly said. "I'll be right behind you, but I'll wait until you're inside."

He opened the back door and grabbed his hat and the large boxy case that held the portable dictaphone. For a brief moment, Molly held eye contact with him. "Good luck, James," she said earnestly.

James returned Molly's gaze and, after a moment, gave the briefest of nods. "Okay," was all he said before closing the door. Molly heard his footsteps recede.

The nod brought the slightest bit of comfort to Molly, but it still stung that James hadn't said more. Of course, Molly understood why.

After a few moments, Molly peeked through the window again. James was standing at the blue door, holding the large case under one arm. The door was then pulled open, and after a brief pause, James disappeared inside.

Now was the time to act. Molly threw off the blanket and quietly exited the car. The remaining sunlight had dissipated, and the air took on an early evening chill. She walked casually but swiftly toward the Owenses' residence. Following Sylvia's instructions, she made her way along the side of the house to the backyard through a quaint wooden gate.

The back of the Owenses' property was cool and shaded. Molly spied the sturdy iron trellis covered with pinkish-white climbing roses Sylvia told her to look out for. The top of the trellis reached nearly to one of the balconies that jutted out from under two matching sets of windows along the back.

With a heave, Molly carefully picked her way up the trellis, being mindful of the thorny branches that sprouted the delicate flowers. At the top of the trellis, she hoisted herself onto the nearest balcony and took a moment to catch her breath. She tightened her gun holster, which had shifted slightly during her climb.

Molly peered through gaps in the curtains that hung over the etched glass doors. Inside, a soft light was glowing from a small lamp perched on a vanity. A large canopy bed with fluffy pillows stood at one end of the room.

Sylvia's room. There was a stirring in Molly's heart. In any other scenario, this moment would be romantically thrilling. But with James somewhere inside with Carl, there was no time to imagine romance. The door to the balcony was unlocked, as Sylvia had promised. Molly slipped inside.

Sylvia's intoxicating aroma filled Molly's senses instantly. A tin of face powder was neatly closed up on the vanity, but the smell was unmistakable. The scent of lilacs that followed Sylvia around must have come from the ornate perfume mister that sat near the face powder tin. Though Molly was alone in the room, Sylvia's presence was everywhere here. At this moment, Molly knew Sylvia would be downstairs with James and Carl, offering them both a beverage.

Over the phone, Sylvia had told Molly how much Carl loved to play the sophisticate whenever meeting someone new. She'd said Carl would want to impress James with his whiskey collection, which would buy Molly a little time to sneak in unobserved.

Molly quietly cracked open the door to the hallway and assessed the layout of the second story of the Owenses' home. From Sylvia's descriptions, she knew that the next room over would be Carl's office. The master bedroom, which Carl had long since taken over as solely his own, was at the end of the hall near the upstairs bathroom. Murmured voices from the first floor floated up the grand staircase to the second-floor landing.

As quiet as she could be, Molly left the safety of Sylvia's room for Carl's office down the hall to her right. She closed the door silently behind her. Carl's office contained a wall of bookshelves, a fireplace with a couple of club chairs posed in front of it, a stately wooden desk, a door that led to a closet, and a balcony identical to the one off of Sylvia's room.

Molly crept quickly to the office's balcony doors. Outside, she found a small, neat pile of rose petals. For a moment, her breath stilled while fluttering filled her belly and she grinned involuntarily. Molly had asked Sylvia to provide something she could toss off the balcony—something Sylvia could see from down below through the sitting room windows as a signal that Molly was in place. But Molly had pictured something less romantic than the pink and white flowers from the trellis she'd just climbed up—a handful of gravel perhaps, or some leaves from an old dead potted plant. Flower petals felt like flirtation, a feeling she couldn't help but smile about.

Molly dumped the petals off the balcony and hoped Sylvia had seen them. At this point, she imagined Sylvia would have just handed Carl and James their whiskey cocktails.

Molly tucked herself into the nook between the balcony doors and the wrought iron railing, where she remained hidden from anyone who would be inside the room. If she peeked, she'd have a clear enough sightline into Carl's office and could hear anything that was said through the glass panels of the balcony doors. It was only a minute or so until she finally heard James and Carl enter the office.

"...need to keep it out of sight," Carl was saying. "I need to catch it all on the recording. Set it up right here, under the desk. Just as you had it in your office. Only we'll hide it better this time." Carl let out a sound that passed for a laugh. Molly imagined James's irritation at the joke and willed him to keep steady.

"Of course," was all James said. It was quiet for a moment, aside from the sounds of the case being opened and the equipment set up. Then there was a tentative knock at the door to the hallway.

"Dammit all," Carl muttered. As Molly heard the hallway door opening, he barked, "What is it?"

"I'd prefer not to see him." It was Sylvia, speaking to Carl near his office door. Molly risked peeking through the curtains to see a glimpse of Sylvia and watch the interaction. "Please? Would you mind answering the door? I just saw him pull up—he'll be knocking any moment. I can imagine he'll only get agitated if he sees me, you know. Might be better for your plans if *you* serve him a drink rather than me."

Smart, Molly thought.

"Hmm," Carl started, "I can't very well have him in a bad mood from the get-go. And lord knows you give people ulcers just by being near them. Fine. Stay out of sight." Through the curtains, Molly saw Carl point at James. "You, hide in here and keep quiet. You can take your drink if you'd like. Just don't spill on my suits." Carl walked over and opened the closet door behind his desk, then shoved aside some suits that crowded the small space.

Oh great, James'll just love that. Molly thought back to the bottle of champagne she'd promised him. That wouldn't cut it anymore. She would need to get him a new Lincoln and a gold bracelet and a pair of diamond cuff links.

Carl then said to Sylvia, "I don't want to see you again for the rest of the night. Leave the men alone. Shouldn't be hard for a deviant like you."

After a confusing few moments of sounds Molly couldn't interpret, the balcony door was cracked open. "Molly?" Sylvia's worried face appeared. Behind her, James peered out to the balcony as well. Carl was nowhere to be seen.

"I'm here." Molly looked back and forth between the two of them, "So...James, Sylvia. Sylvia, James. I guess you've met by now."

"Yes." Sylvia smiled warmly at James. "Thank you again, James."

James looked from Molly to Sylvia, his gruff face softening slightly. "Oh. Well...I...I'm happy to help."

From downstairs, they all heard the front door open and close, followed by loud, jovial banter being exchanged between Carl and Chief King. "Here we go," James said to Molly and Sylvia. He looked at Molly once more and said, "Wish us luck."

Molly shot James a warm smile. "Luck." He disappeared into the office closet and Molly began to close the balcony door to conceal herself again. But before she could shut the door, Sylvia quickly reached for Molly's wrist, gripping it tightly.

"Molly...," was all she could say. Her eyes were wide, terrified.

Molly gently placed a hand over Sylvia's. She remembered suddenly when they were in this same position not long ago. Sylvia distraught in her office, Molly attempting to calm the beautiful stranger whose story didn't make sense. It was only now that Molly knew how wrong she had been. She should have listened to Sylvia in the first place.

"It will be fine. I promise." Molly squeezed her hand once more and closed herself back into her hiding spot. From her vantage point, she watched Sylvia quickly leave through the door to the hallway.

It was only a short time before Carl entered the office again, this time with Lonnie King. Lonnie's police uniform was slightly wrinkled.

"Have a seat there," Carl said with a smile. Lonnie took the armchair across from Carl's desk, adjusting the gun at his hip as he sat down. Carl perched on the edge of his desk, swirling his glass of whiskey. "Tell me, King. How's business?"

Lonnie guffawed. "Hoo boy! This new gig we've got going on is something else, I tell you what! The boys couldn't be happier than when I tell 'em to go hog wild on the fairies."

"That so?"

Through the curtain, Molly watched Carl calmly

observing as Lonnie slurped his drink. After a moment Carl spoke again. "You happy with the arrangement, then?"

"Oh, you bet. You know as well as I do, those places need to be shut down anyhow. No good can come from those kinds congregating together. It ain't right." Lonnie's brow suddenly furrowed. "You and I both know the trouble it causes. Fucking faggots and lady faggots. If I could burn all those places down, I would." He guffawed again. "You know, when I'm busting those joints, sometimes I can't even tell which are the men and which are the women!"

"Then why the hell are you trying to shake me out, King?" Carl said with an eerie calm.

What is he doing? Molly snuck a look through the window again. *That's no way to get a man to spill his secrets. He hardly warmed him up!*

Lonnie frowned again and looked directly at Carl. "Shake you out? For what? I ain't shaking nobody out, Owens. What's got your ass chapped?"

"You do, you son of a bitch." At this, Carl sprang to his feet and Lonnie quickly followed suit. For a moment the two men simply stared at each other. Molly's heart raced as she watched from the balcony. If things got heated between Lonnie and Carl, she wasn't sure what she would do. James was still hidden in the closet, listening to all of this. Sylvia was somewhere else in the house, as far as Molly knew. Hopefully away from this appalling conversation.

As long as James and Sylvia were okay, she'd just have

to be patient to see how things played out. All Carl and Lonnie had to do was talk. The machine would catch it all, and she and James could act as witnesses if Mayor Booker needed any more proof.

"The game's up, King. I know about your plan to try to rat me out to that private dick!"

"My plan to *what*? You're talking crazy! You know as well as I do this was all *your* idea in the first place. 'To get back at the girls,' you said. 'Show 'em who runs this town,' you said. I'm just 'the hired help,' remember? *The brawn to your brain.* Your words again. It's none of my business if you fancy yourself to be mayor someday. I said I'd vote for you, didn't I? What more do you want? All I been doing's my own damn job. You want to cut me checks for it every once in a while, that's your own damn business!"

Suddenly, Carl rushed to the closet where James was hiding. "Aha! Tell that to your friend here!" With a flourish, Carl opened the closet door wide to reveal a stunned and red-faced James.

"Hey, what's the big idea?" Lonnie exclaimed in confusion. "You got a spy in here? Who's this?"

James emerged from the closet, his face damp, looking slightly delirious. His whiskey glass was empty, and he awkwardly set it on Carl's desk. Molly could see that James was sweating through his suit. She wished he'd had a gun on him. But he refused to ever carry one, even unloaded as a prop when playing detective.

Molly released the snap on her holster and, for the first time in years, pulled her gun out, ready to fire. She put a hand on the small brass doorknob of the balcony door but remained hidden for now, peering through the curtains.

"Aw, don't give me that crap, King. I know you hired him. And sent those phony letters too! Like I wouldn't see through that after we faked the one for Sylvia. I told you that shit wouldn't work on her, dumb as she is. And it sure as hell didn't work on me. I hired you to kill those fags and goddamn it, you're going to do it!"

Lonnie regarded Carl with a bemused smile. He chugged the last of his whiskey, then set the glass down loudly on the desk. "You're losing it, Owens. You really are. Sylvia's got you messed up for sure. You should have taken care of her long ago, just like I did with Jane. As for this dumb son of a bitch…I never seen him before in my whole goddamn life."

Carl paused, then looked back and forth between James and Lonnie. "You…you really don't know him?"

Lonnie looked James up and down. "No way. I'd remember that mug for sure. Who is he?"

Now Carl turned to face James as well. Both Lonnie and Carl stood with their backs to Molly and the balcony doors.

"Well, asshole?" Carl said to James. "You heard *Chief* King. Who are you?"

Outside, Molly's heart raced. James was in a bind, and she needed to help. On the other hand, she didn't want to underestimate James. Maybe he could handle this and if Molly came in now, she'd blow the whole thing.

But no, she didn't want to risk James being in danger any longer. It was time to step in.

At the same moment that Molly flung open the balcony door and burst into the room with her gun raised, Sylvia also emerged just as suddenly through the hallway door. Both women yelled simultaneously. Sylvia shouted, "I hired him!" while Molly called out, "It's me you want!"

Carl and Lonnie looked bug-eyed back and forth between Sylvia and Molly.

"Who…what…?" was all Carl could get out.

"The hell's going on around here?" Lonnie shouted. He drew his weapon but couldn't decide who to point the gun at—James, Sylvia, Carl, Molly. He settled on grabbing the person closest to him to hold hostage. It was Sylvia.

"Somebody better start talking or the dyke gets it," Lonnie snarled. He had one beefy arm hooked around Sylvia, pinning her arms to her sides, his gun held to her head.

Molly aimed at Lonnie's head. "Drop it, Chief."

"Who in the good goddamn are you?" Carl growled at Molly. "And what the fuck are you doing on my balcony?"

"We met yesterday at my office. Don't you remember?"

"The secretary?" Carl frowned at James, growing angrier in his confusion. "What the hell is she talking about?"

James just shrugged.

"Molly Malone, private detective. You're in big trouble, Councilman. You too, Chief. I know all about the murders. I know all about your schemes and plans. The two of you will be wearing stripes in no time. We have all the evidence we need."

"We?" Carl shot a look at Sylvia. "Sylvie, baby. Is this

another of your little friends?" With a laugh, he glared at his wife. "You found someone else to warm you on the cold nights alone?"

Lonnie barked a laugh, too, and jostled Sylvia around in his grip. "A dyke detective! Imagine that!"

"I'm warning you, Chief," Molly said. "Drop it and let her go."

"Not on your life." Lonnie made to drag Sylvia out of the room, but suddenly James sprang into action, tackling Lonnie and knocking Sylvia free.

"Run!" Molly shouted. But Sylvia didn't need the instruction. She took off down the hall and Carl bolted after her.

James and Lonnie scuffled on the floor. Fists and elbows landed with grunts from both of them. Molly didn't have a clean shot to intervene. Then she saw an opening and aimed her weapon.

But she was too late. A blast rang out, but it wasn't from her gun. Lonnie had fired.

Molly's ears rang and her vision blurred. It took her a moment to register what had happened. Then she saw James stumble down the hallway, clutching his side and groaning.

"*James!*"

"Hold it right there, dyke bitch." Lonnie trained his gun on her. In the chaos, Molly had lost her concentration and her gun dangled uselessly from her hand. She had no choice but to drop it and put her hands up.

From downstairs, the front door slammed open. Lonnie blocked the office doorway with his body and smiled wickedly at her. "You don't stand a chance with any of this. Who would believe *you* over me? I'm the goddamn chief of police."

"Then you should know that what you're doing is illegal."

"*You* should know that all those fairy clubs are illegal. Not to mention wrong."

Molly gritted her teeth. "Killing people is *also* illegal, you dumb son of a bitch. *Not to mention wrong.*"

"Not when you're me," Lonnie said with a grin. And for the second time, he pulled the trigger of his gun.

Molly winced, but his gun had jammed.

"Fuck!" He turned his gun to the side to inspect it. In his moment of hesitation, Molly bolted for the balcony. The shock of the fresh night air let her know how much she'd been sweating and how hot that room had gotten in such a short period of time.

She looked for a way down, but there was no nearby iron trellis like there was from Sylvia's balcony next door. It was a straight shot to the patio and shrubbery ten feet below. Molly quickly climbed to the outside of the balcony railing and lowered herself as far down as she could hang. After the briefest moment of hesitation, she let go.

She landed with a thud in a bush near the brick patio. Her right elbow crunched painfully beneath her. Above her, Lonnie's shadow appeared briefly on the balcony, but she quickly rolled out of his sightline.

After she was sure the coast was clear, she assessed the damage to her elbow. The barest movement of her right arm sent a shock of pain through her body. Gritting her teeth against the pain, she exited the backyard as quickly as she dared.

By the time she passed through the wooden gate she'd first entered the side yard from, she saw Lonnie's police car speeding away. One of the Owenses' cars was gone from the driveway too. Closer to the street she saw a trail of blood leading out the front door and down the sidewalk to where James had parked Molly's car.

James was slumped in the driver's seat, the car door hanging open. Forgetting the pain of her likely broken elbow, Molly rushed to him.

CHAPTER
SIXTEEN

If James dies, I'll never forgive myself.

James's skin was pale, sweaty. His breath was shallow, but it was there. He groaned as Molly pushed him to the passenger seat. "I'm going to get you help," she said, unsure he could even hear her. With a glance back at the Owenses' house, she saw the front door was still wide open and the lights were on inside. She couldn't very well leave things that way. Though it was dark now, any passing neighbor could be curious about the open front door, not to mention the unmistakable drops of blood. "I'll be right back. James? Can you hear me? I'm coming right back and I'll get you some help."

Molly reached the front door but paused before pulling it shut. All the evidence was upstairs. Everything they'd been working for. The recordings. If she left them for Carl to retrieve, this would all be for nothing. She had to take everything with her.

She rushed through Sylvia and Carl's living room,

unavoidably following the trail of James's blood that led up the stairs and back to the office on the second floor. She was stopped cold for a brief moment as she remembered the sound of the gunshot that had created the pool of blood before her. It was as glistening and vibrant as anything she'd ever seen.

With her one good arm, Molly retrieved the dicta-phone, which had recorded the whole horrifying thing. As she gathered the machine, a stack of papers caught her attention.

The neat penmanship at the top of the page read *Acceptance Speech*.

Molly remembered what Sylvia had said. *He's been working on this speech…I'm sure it's connected.*

She scanned the first few words:

Given the untimely and devastating assassination of our beloved mayor Martin Booker, I am both grieved and honored to accept the nomination from my peers for the role of mayor of San Francisco…

"Holy cats," Molly whispered. *An assassination plot?* Was all this part of a plan to get rid of Mayor Booker? Both Sylvia and Lonnie had mentioned that Carl had a plan to become mayor someday.

Molly shoved the pages of the written speech into the dictaphone case. Fluttering down from the desk came another familiar document. It was the original list of club addresses that Chief King had a mimeographed copy of in his office. She grabbed that, too, and registered now that the list had been written by Carl in the first place—the handwritten speech shared the same neat penmanship as the list.

Before leaving the room, Molly picked up her gun from the floor and, realizing her shooting hand was now useless, did her best to refit her holster to the other side. She hadn't shot with her left hand in years.

The heavy case banged against her legs as she lugged it down the staircase with her left arm. Molly's right elbow was now swelling dangerously, but she had no time to think about it or slow her pace.

With James slumped over in the passenger seat—moving him over had been quite a feat, especially with an injured arm—Molly sped through the crooked streets, mindful of police cars but gunning the engine at every turn when she could. The hospital wasn't far. She glanced at James every few seconds. If he didn't make it, Lewis's last anniversary with him would have been ruined by Molly's stupid insistence that he attend a policeman's banquet, only to listen to anti-gay slurs and idiotic fear. She knew James would never forgive her for any of this. If he lived that long.

Molly took a corner sharply. In the backseat, the dicta-phone case thumped as it toppled over with the momentum of the turn. Had she really wasted a few precious moments to run back inside and grab the stupid thing when James was sitting in her car bleeding his life away? *Stupid girl. Stupid, stupid, stupid.*

Suddenly James pulled himself up to a sitting position. "Leave me here," he wheezed. The hospital was still half a block away.

"James!" Molly almost slammed on the brakes at the sound of his voice. He groaned miserably. "You can't be seen near me. Not with that gun on you. There'll be questions." He spoke each word slowly with firm insistence.

"Never mind all that! You need help. I'll—"

"You'll *get the fuck out of here* is what you'll do, Molly!" James's face was even whiter than before. "I'll have them call Lewis. *You need to go.* Get Paula. Go anywhere. *Just get away from me.*"

Without another word, Molly pulled the car to the side of the road. Before she could make her way to the other side of the car, James had opened his door and stood up as well as he could.

"*Go*, goddammit!" He then folded to the ground with a painful grunt.

Halfway down the block, some hospital orderlies chatted near the empty parking bay. They turned toward the sound, not sure what they were seeing yet: a man on the ground, a frantic woman hovering above him, a car idling with both doors open. They grabbed a nearby stretcher and then began to run toward James and Molly.

Molly didn't wait for another instruction but promptly closed the now-bloody passenger door and sped off. In her rearview mirror, she saw the orderlies reach James and begin to load him onto the stretcher.

Speeding away, Molly found herself wailing. James was hurt, maybe dying. Lewis would never speak to her again, of course. Carl must have made off with Sylvia, to who knows where. Lonnie was on the loose. And Molly was alone. With a stupid injured arm and nowhere to turn.

Only a week before, her life had been peaceful. Then Sylvia showed up to the office, and Molly had forced James to attend the policeman's banquet. From there, everything seemed to snowball.

Sylvia Owens. There was a pang in Molly's heart and a catch in her throat thinking about Sylvia. For a moment she was angry at letting herself get distracted by her in the first place. And where was she now? Whisked away by Carl, and Molly had no way to know where he'd taken her. With a sickening shock, she remembered Lonnie's words to Carl: *You should have taken care of her...like I did with Jane.* Wherever Sylvia was, Molly couldn't help her now.

She took a few steadying breaths. *Get it together, Malone.*

While working with Thomas Parker years ago, Molly had been impressed with his ability to keep poised in stressful situations. He could have been a mess inside for all Molly knew—but outwardly he appeared to be completely in control of any situation, no matter how dire. That was something Molly had always respected about Thomas. Molly remembered Thomas running past her car, a grief-stricken look on his tear-stained face. What did it mean? What had happened that had left even Thomas so shattered?

In any case, going to Thomas for help now was out of the question. Whatever was going on with Thomas, he wasn't someone Molly could turn to. Not anymore.

She'd give anything to go back to that quiet night at Whiskers.

"I have to get to Paula," Molly said aloud in her car. Even though the Fazio family had refused her warnings, even though they'd refused to help Walter Newton when he asked for help, Paula was still in danger. Perhaps even more so now. Molly may have mangled everything else, but she could still try to save Paula.

That just meant one thing: working with Valentino Fazio.

CHAPTER
SEVENTEEN

Molly headed straight for Whiskers. She didn't care what Paula or Natalia or Valentino Fazio said, they had to believe her this time. At the door, she rapped out the secret knock: *tap tap-tap*.

There was Natalia, working security once again. "I need to talk to your father," Molly said straightaway.

"What's wrong, honey?" Natalia said with a furrowed brow. "You look like you've seen some shit."

Molly gripped one of Natalia's arms firmly and looked very intently into her face. "I need to see Valentino immediately."

Natalia's face changed. "Oh, I see. He's here. In the back."

With a nod of thanks, Molly made her way through the club. It wasn't terribly late in the evening, but several regulars were already there, sipping drinks and swaying to the music. She saw Paula watching her from behind the bar as she fixed drinks, curious. Molly passed through club-goers who were dancing and happily conversing. She cradled her right arm carefully. Paula served the batch of drinks to her customers, then hurried to join Molly before she made it to the door to the back hallways.

"What happened?" Paula said, eyeing Molly's arm.

Molly didn't answer and Paula didn't ask again. They swiftly made their way down the long narrow hallway toward the back room.

"I was thinking about what you said," Paula started. "About the family's arrangement with the cops…"

Molly was beginning to feel feverish from the pain. "And?"

"It's not really up to me…but I'm inclined to believe you."

Molly grunted a laugh, then wiped a hand across her damp forehead. "Why is that?"

"In the years we've known each other, we've let each other be, right? Haven't meddled in each other's…business. Haven't made a fuss. But you took a risk coming here. Talking to Uncle Val. You wouldn't have done that if it wasn't serious."

"Right." Molly was relieved to hear that Paula believed her.

"I'm sorry I didn't see that right away. It wasn't until after you'd gone that I thought more about it. But I never liked that guy—King. The way he leers when he's here picking up his money. Something about him always set me off. And it's not just because he's a cop."

"I think he killed his wife."

Paula's eyes got big. "The cop did?"

"I think so. Because he caught her with a woman."

Paula shook her head. "Wow. Figures. That's a damn shame. Did you know her? She ever come here?"

"I didn't know her. She'd been with…a friend of mine. Few years ago."

At the end of the hallway, the door to the small living room area was partly open. "Uncle Val?" Paula called as they approached. "It's Molly. She needs help."

Valentino Fazio appeared in the doorway, as slick and put together as the first time Molly saw him. "Molly Malone! Are you hurt? Come sit!"

Once settled on the couch, Molly told them everything that had happened since she last saw them. She described what she'd learned about both Lonnie and Carl and how her plan had backfired. "I don't know when, but they *will* be coming after Paula. You need to make sure she's safe and that everyone in that front room is safe. You need to be on alert. Lonnie King can't be trusted."

After she'd finished speaking, there was silence for a few moments.

"Molly Malone," Valentino began, "the last time we spoke, I listened to your concerns. I like to think I will always listen to the concerns of those who Paula or Natalia consider friends." He leaned closer to Molly. "But I am afraid you have not understood how limited my extension of love and caretaking truly is. As a matter of fact, I fear you are overstepping into business that does not concern you. And although I am not yet sure of your motive, I do know that your interest in the Fazio family is…inappropriate. I need to warn you of this. That to tell me, *Valentino Fazio*, about what I *need to do* is quite a dangerous choice of words. Molly Malone, for some reason I simply adore you. Which is why I must for the last time tell you to *kindly* keep your—"

But Valentino couldn't finish. With a loud crash, Lonnie King burst through the door of the backroom with his gun raised.

He fixed his aim on the first face his eyes landed on: Paula's.

In a flash, Molly's left hand reached for her gun as her right elbow stabbed white hot with the sudden movement. Taking the briefest of seconds to aim, she fired.

Lonnie's body shot sideways against the wall, where he slumped with a scream as loud as the gun's firing.

For a moment the room was silent, filled only by the hot metal vapors of gunpowder. Valentino, Natalia, and Paula all looked at Molly, whose gun was still smoking.

Then came a groan from the floor.

"You shot me, you dyke bitch!" Lonnie writhed on the ground.

Valentino locked eyes with Molly, and she knew at once that he finally believed her.

She also knew she needed to tend to Lonnie. Much as she hated him, she couldn't let him bleed out. She wanted him in jail, not dead. She'd successfully stopped him from killing Paula, but now he was the one in need of saving. She rushed to Lonnie's side. But with only one usable arm, she had no strength to stop the bleeding from his shoulder, where Molly's bullet had shot clean through.

"He needs a hospital," Molly said firmly to the Fazios. But Paula only looked away from Molly's gaze.

Natalia and Valentino exchanged a look Molly couldn't interpret.

"Paula, see to your customers," Valentino said softly. "Drinks on the house tonight."

With a final look at Molly, Paula grabbed two bottles of whiskey from the shelves and headed back to the front of the house.

Molly's elbow throbbed. She felt nauseated from the pain and overwhelmed by the events of the evening. Lonnie's warm blood pulsed over her left hand as she attempted unsuccessfully to stop the blood flowing from his injury.

Once Paula was out of the room, Natalia gently pulled Molly away from Lonnie, then expertly propped him up against the wall, despite Lonnie's loud groans and protests.

Valentino gave Molly a clean, neatly folded bar towel to wipe the blood from her hand. With her right arm nearly useless, she only succeeded in smearing most of the blood away.

"Chief King, I am surprised at you," Valentino said calmly. "My friend Molly Malone has told me some very disturbing information. At first, I admit that I did not believe her. Because why would a man in such as position as yourself risk so much for a few measly dollars?" Valentino crouched down to be on eye level with Lonnie. Lonnie's face grew whiter and glistened in the low lights of the room's lamps.

My friend Molly Malone. Given everything else that had taken place over the previous few hours, such a phrase shouldn't have been as chilling as it was. Molly stood frozen near the cool walls of the basement bar's back room. Lonnie's blood began to get sticky along her arm and the sleeve of her blouse. Her throat tightened against the threat of vomiting from the pain she was in, the scene in front of her, and her worry for James and Sylvia.

"Do you know what it is to go behind the back of Valentino Fazio?" Valentino arose and kicked Lonnie in the side with a force so powerful that Lonnie's screams wheezed inward as he gulped a breath and slumped over. After a moment, Natalia propped Lonnie against the wall again.

"This city does not belong to you." Valentino gave Lonnie another kick. This time when he slumped to the floor, Natalia didn't bother picking him up. "Whiskers does not belong to you." *Kick.* "A man who goes by both names of *Chief* and *King* but does nothing..."—*kick*—"...to deserve those titles is the truest kind of coward."

"Stop! Please!" Lonnie screeched. "It wasn't my idea!"

"Not your idea?" Valentino chuckled softly. "There is nothing quite so weak as a man who takes action on something he doesn't believe in. A man who has no morals of his own but only acts on the will of others is a waste of God's earthly space. Which is why you deserve my pity. I give you now a moment of respite before we're done." Valentino grabbed Lonnie's head and aimed his thick, sweating face toward Molly. "You see her? This is Molly Malone. *Friend of Valentino Fazio.* In your final moments, I will allow you to look upon her as an example of the kind of person you could never be. Someone kind, someone loyal, someone good. May you think of her as the kind of man you have failed to be, when you are standing at the gates of hell."

And with that, Valentino Fazio pulled a gleaming knife from inside his suit jacket and slid it deep into Lonnie's heart. Molly looked away. She couldn't bear to see Lonnie's shocked, white face and bulging eyes any longer.

For several moments, the room was silent but for the gasping breaths of a dying man. Finally, even that sound stopped. Natalia, Molly, and Valentino looked at each other in the stillness.

In the silence of the room, the faint sounds of the oblivious club-goers trickled softly in. If anyone had heard the gunshot or the rest of the disturbance, perhaps they were now so distracted by the free whiskey that it was promptly forgotten. In any case, no one charged through the door wondering what the commotion had been. There were only sounds of the joyful greeting of friends, boisterous conversation, and the faint melody of a lovely song.

CHAPTER
EIGHTEEN

Detective Thomas Parker sat stiffly on a park bench next to none other than Molly Malone. She was no longer the fresh graduate of secretarial school that she had been when they'd first started working together. He'd been surprised, but not upset, that she'd called him at the station and requested to talk to him. But given the missing pieces in his own investigation, he couldn't say no.

"You said you have information?" was all Thomas offered as a greeting. He'd prepared himself as well as he could for seeing her again, and for speaking to her this time. But once she'd appeared in the dappled sunlight of Golden Gate Park, the hot shame of how he'd treated her over a year ago come flooding back.

"First of all, I'm not here to talk about us, about our friendship. I know you don't want to talk about what happened between us and that's fine. Let's just move on from all that," Molly said. "What I have to tell you is more important anyway. Sound okay?"

As usual, Molly didn't pussyfoot around. Thomas had forgotten how much he appreciated that about her. "Alright."

Molly nodded, rubbing her shoulder above the bulky white cast that kept her right elbow at a stiff angle. "I know you're on the vice squad now. And that you've been involved with the raids. I'm not going to ask you why. But I will say this…" She turned toward Thomas and leaned over the heavy dictaphone case she had set between them when she arrived. She looked exhausted. "I know that Carl Owens and Lonnie King were—*are*—in business together and that their methods are…less than legal."

Thomas looked sharply at her.

"I also know there was money exchanged. I have what I believe would be admissible as evidence in a plot to assassinate Mayor Booker." With her good arm, she pulled a stack of files from a side pocket of the dictaphone case. "Here's the evidence I've collected, along with my statement."

Thomas flipped through the documents, carefully studying each one. "Did you type this transcription?"

"I did." Molly gestured at the cast on her right arm. "Took me a hell of a long time. A copy of the recordings is in the box there. I have the originals protected."

"What's the motive?"

"Owens and King had a personal vendetta against the clubs because their wives had been two-timing them…"

Thomas cocked an eyebrow.

"With each other," Molly finished.

"Ah."

"What happened at the Hot Spot raid? When you ran."

The sudden question made hot tears sting Thomas's eyes. His mouth filled with saliva as though he might be sick. He clenched his eyes shut at the memories of that night. The terror of the people in the bar, the rock in his gut as he made arrests. And finally, the look on Lonnie's face when he shot and killed the club owner in cold blood, out of sight of the other officers—all but Thomas, who stayed inside while the others marched out. On any other day, it could have been Thomas being arrested by his fellow officers. The thought paralyzed him; he was stuck in place while the rooms emptied out, his still figure ignored or unseen by his boisterous fellow officers who gleefully made arrests.

As the room had emptied, Thomas crept to the back reaches of the Hot Spot's interior, fighting the clenching in his gut, the pain in his chest, the fear that crept in from all sides.

Then Chief King, who hadn't seen Thomas crouched in the corner, pointed his gun into the open door of a back office that was out of Thomas's sightline.

"*No-please-God-no-please-why!*" came the cry from someone in the room.

Then the blast from Lonnie's gun. Thomas jumped up, but he was too late. King turned away in time to see Thomas standing near him, stricken. "Ah, Parker! Stay with me, will ya? Gotta wait for the ambulance now. The others will go in the wagon. Hell of a night, huh?" The chief clapped Thomas on the back, jovially, not seeing or not caring that Thomas only looked on in horror at the dead body of Walter Newton.

Thomas recounted to Molly what he'd seen. All the frightful details, admitting the way he'd hidden, the way he was struck frozen and couldn't help. When he finished, he couldn't tell what Molly might be thinking of him. Shame? Judgement? He mentally willed Molly to break the silence. *Say something, dammit.*

But Molly just listened quietly, offering no absolution… but maybe a chance at redemption. After a moment, she pointed to a handwritten list among the documents she'd brought along. "Whiskers was going to be the next one."

Thomas considered this. He was silent for a moment before tentatively asking, "Do you know what happened to the chief?" He watched Molly's face carefully. When she hesitated to respond, he said, "I trust you. I know that sounds strange after what I put you through. But I trust your instincts. I know you're friendly with some members of the Fazio family, given their…*connection* to Whiskers. I suspect they know where the chief is. And I imagine you might know as well."

"Why do you suspect the Fazios?"

"Natalia Fazio paid me a visit the other day. Since I'm next in line on the vice squad, she wanted to make sure I'd cooperate with them. And since she also knows me from Whiskers, I didn't have much choice but to agree. Seems

I'm under their thumb now too. And another thing. I talked with a friend of yours who showed up at the hospital with a gunshot wound."

"You talked to James?"

"His partner called me. I visited them both right after his surgery."

"How did he look?"

Thomas looked at Molly, surprised. "You haven't seen him?"

She shook her head. "He doesn't want to talk to me right now. It's my fault he got shot in the first place."

Thomas nodded and allowed a moment of space for what Molly said. "He looked rough. But okay. Doc said it was a clean shot that should heal nicely. Lost a lot of blood, but he'll be no worse for wear."

Sunshine pooled around them as the midmorning sunlight found gaps in the upper branches of the old oak trees.

"Why did James want to talk to you?"

"He wanted to tell me the chief shot him. At Carl Owens's house, no less. He said he was visiting a friend in her home when an altercation broke out. I knew you'd have more details. The only thing I can't figure is what happened to the chief. No one can account for his whereabouts after leaving Carl Owens's place. Then when the Fazios stepped in after the fact, it seemed easy enough to put two and two together. But I want to hear it straight. Did the Fazios kill Lonnie King?"

Thomas watched Molly as she considered how to

answer. Finally, she nodded. "Yes. They killed him. I don't know what they did with his body." Molly related the details of that night in the backroom of Whiskers. How she'd tried for the second time to warn Paula. How Lonnie had come in with his service pistol drawn. How Molly shot first in order to save her friend. Finally, she described Valentino's knife and what he did with it.

"After that, they all but shoved me out the door. With a promise that they'd be in touch, whatever that might mean. Valentino insisted I go to a specific hospital for this." She held up the bulky cast. "He said they wouldn't ask any questions."

Thomas considered this. The cast that encased Molly's elbow and forearm looked perfectly professional—no indication of a half-assed hack job—which meant there was a hospital somewhere in the city that catered to the whims of the notorious Don Fazio. He let out a heavy sigh. What else was happening in this town that he didn't know about?

And now Molly, his old friend and former colleague, was involved with the Mafia, seemingly by accident. Same as he was. "Are you scared? Be honest, Molly."

She shrugged with her one good shoulder, her brow furrowed. "I'm...uneasy."

Thomas nodded. "That makes two of us."

"Thanks for meeting with me," she said abruptly. "This investigation could have been easier with you by my side the whole time. Like the old days."

There was a moment of uncomfortable silence that

Molly refused to break. Thomas knew she deserved an explanation for how he'd treated her. He now understood it was finally time.

"You have to understand how it is for me," Thomas began. "I have children. A *wife*. Think how it would be if she found out. It would devastate her."

"Did you think I would have said something?" Molly tried to catch his eye.

Thomas shook his head. "I didn't think about that. All I could think was that I couldn't risk it. I'd been terrified of going out that night anyway. With Edwin Atherton hardly out of town and not long gone, I knew I was taking a risk even going to places like Whiskers. Then when I saw you…I took it as a sign that I was on the wrong path. That I was putting my career and my family in danger. I knew that if I got you transferred somewhere else in the station, at least you'd still have a job. I thought if I could keep you out of my sight, I wouldn't have to think about what to do. I knew if we talked about it, I'd have to make a decision. Keep doing what I'm doing; tell my wife; don't tell my wife and just leave her…there's no good option. And I wasn't ready to make a decision. I'm still not."

Molly abruptly pulled Thomas into a hug. The heft of her cast pressed into his ribs. He wrapped his arms around her as well. After a moment, they parted, their eyes watery.

Thomas lit a cigarette with shaking hands. "That night at the Hot Spot—you said you were there? I didn't see you."

"You taught me well."

Thomas smiled softly at that.

"I was across the street. Saw it all go down, but I wasn't inside. I was parked in the alley with Carl Owens's wife.

Thomas laughed. A truly joyful laugh that astonished him in its strength. "Molly Malone, you old so-and-so."

Molly smiled. "It wasn't like that. She's a client."

Thomas felt a pleasant stirring in his chest. Given their previously held secrets, he and Molly had never before discussed their romantic lives. But now that they were, they felt like easy friends again.

"Not like that?" Thomas was dubious.

"Maybe a *little* like that." It was Molly's turn to laugh. "But she's a client first."

In Molly's good-natured grin, Thomas remembered the rapport they'd shared years ago. "What is she second?" he asked, keeping the joke going. "Mrs. Carl Owens?"

Molly thought for a moment. "Not that." She stood, preparing to leave. "She's just herself."

Thomas stood quickly to stop Molly before leaving. "You should talk to a lawyer, Molly. I know a good one, if you'll accept my help. He's...a friend."

He quickly scribbled something on a scrap of paper. Molly inspected it.

After a moment, Thomas blurted out. "You saw him once, actually. Before all this happened—when I saw you a few weeks ago at Whiskers. The night before the policeman's banquet? I was there with Joseph."

Molly brightened. A goofy smile lit up her face. "The man in the checked coat! I remember. He's a lawyer?"

"Not just any lawyer. He's the district attorney. He'll do everything he can to take Carl Owens down, especially since the chief is dead. Booker will want someone to pay for what happened. Last man standing—unfortunately for Councilman Owens, he's it."

CHAPTER
NINETEEN

In the days that followed the horrific events in her home, Sylvia grew increasingly sick with worry. Once the altercation broke out and she'd made a break for it down the stairs, Carl was too quick on her heels for her to make an escape.

As Carl shoved her into the car, they'd both heard a gunshot from inside the house, which caused Carl only the slightest moment of pause. But of course, neither of them could know who had done the shooting, nor if anyone had been injured or perhaps killed. But coming home to a pool of blood leading out the front door only confirmed Sylvia's worst fears.

That night, Carl had driven maniacally for an hour without stopping—even at stop signs—with Sylvia in the passenger seat. She couldn't tell where they were going, and it seemed Carl didn't have much of a plan either. He seemed to drive just to drive. All along the way he ranted at her. But she barely heard a word he'd said for the terror she felt from the sound of the gunshot.

If Molly or James had been killed because of her, she would never be able to forgive herself. On the other hand, perhaps Lonnie had been the one to get shot. In which case, there were more worries: What would be the repercussions for someone who'd killed the police chief? With no way to know whose blood was on her floor or what exactly had happened after Carl whisked her away, Sylvia was nearly driven mad.

Back at home, Carl and Sylvia had sidestepped the bloody trail that led out of their home. Without pausing his momentum, Carl all but dragged Sylvia upstairs—his firm grip on her upper arms left dark bruises. In Sylvia's bedroom, Carl disconnected the phone line, locked her balcony door and tucked the small key in his pocket, and then locked her in her bedroom suite. Sylvia was trapped with no way to call for help.

One morning a couple of days after the incident, Carl delivered the daily plate of food he so graciously provided so she wouldn't starve to death. He'd made her stand across the room so she couldn't make a break for it when he opened the door to set her food inside.

As he slid the tray of food into the room, there was a loud banging and shouting on the front door. Carl and Sylvia locked eyes. "Not one sound from you," he growled before closing her in and locking the door once more.

Sylvia's only windows to the outside world faced the backyard, so she wasn't able to look for whose car might be out front. She hurried to her bedroom door and listened as intently as she could.

For a moment she heard only muffled voices, but very quickly, she heard Carl's voice raised in a shout: "—quite preposterous!" And then: "Unhand me, I tell you!" Then there were the voices of several men speaking at once.

Though she still didn't know who was downstairs, the fact that Carl was displeased gave Sylvia courage enough to make some noise. She banged on her bedroom door and yelled as loudly as she could, "Up here! He has me trapped!"

Soon she heard a rush of footsteps up the stairs and her bedroom door was flung open. "There you are," said the handsome blond man in the police uniform. "Detective Thomas Parker. You must be Sylvia? Molly will be so relieved."

"Molly? She's okay?"

"Yes, she's just fine," Thomas said warmly. "A little banged up. She's worried sick about you, though. Are you alright? Injured at all?"

Sylvia shook her head. "Just glad to know she's okay. What about James?"

"He'll be alright too. Recovering at the moment, but he'll make it." Thomas regarded her kindly.

"Oh, thank God." Sylvia collapsed onto the bench that sat at her vanity. Then she remembered Lonnie King. "What about—"

But the officer stopped her before she could finish. "I'm sorry to rush you, but your husband is under arrest. We're taking him to the station now and we'd like to get a statement from you too. How quickly can you be ready to leave?"

"The station?"

With a quick glance downstairs, Thomas stepped a few more feet into Sylvia's bedroom suite. He spoke quietly. "You're not in any trouble. Molly handed me the evidence implicating both your husband and Lonnie King in quite a number of crimes. I can assure you, Mrs.—uh, *Sylvia*—it's all over now." Thomas glanced again to the doorway. The voices of the other police officers had quieted, and Sylvia no longer heard Carl's protestations. "I think they've already taken Mr. Owens in another car. However, we will be doing a quick sweep of the house before we go. Our warrant is limited for now. But Mr. Owens's office is a main target. If there's anything in the home that…that *you'd rather we not find*, I'd suggest you retrieve it quickly."

There was only one thing in the house she wanted to keep safe: Jane's letters. As soon as Detective Parker left her room, she retrieved Jane's two letters along with the third forged letter from under her pillow.

On the drive to the station in Detective Parker's police car, Sylvia was briefed on what had happened since she'd been locked away. "Molly was so worried about you," he said again. He explained that a good friend of his was the district attorney and would be representing the city in Carl's trial "Joseph Beech," Detective Parker said. "He's… one of us. I met him at the Hot Spot years ago."

From then on, everything happened so fast. Molly was standing outside the police station to greet them when they arrived. The sight of Molly's arm in a cast brought startled tears to Sylvia's eyes. She grabbed Molly in the most tender hug she could manage while feeling too many things she couldn't name. But they didn't have long before Sylvia was whisked away again to give a statement to Joseph Beech, Esquire.

Now, nearly two months later, Sylvia sat sweating in the courtroom. Thomas had already reported on the raids of the clubs as directed by the initiative headed by Lonnie and Carl. "We were told to go hard on them," Detective Thomas Parker had said on the stand. "In fact, under the leadership of King and Owens, we were encouraged to break protocol and incite violence at every turn."

Now it was Sylvia's turn to be questioned. "And how long did he keep you locked in the room?" Joseph Beech asked her.

"As soon as we returned from that late-night drive, he locked me in. I would guess that was around two in the morning on Saturday. And then I was trapped there over Saturday night, and Sunday night, and Monday night. It was only when Detective Parker opened the door for me that I could get out. That was around nine fifteen in the morning the following Tuesday." Sylvia took a sip of water, then looked into the crowd of trial spectators. Molly was among them, offering a soft and encouraging smile the whole time.

Joseph nodded gravely at Sylvia's words and thought

for a moment before asking a follow-up question. "At what point in the evening's events did you recognize that your ability to leave the situation had ended? That is to say, when did you stop being in control of what happened to you?"

Sylvia considered. "I suppose when he grabbed me, after I'd started to run away. Around nine p.m."

"Very interesting," the attorney mused with a subtle wink to Sylvia. He'd prepared her for this line of questioning, which he'd explained before the trial began. "If I'm understanding correctly, between the hours of nine p.m. that Friday and nine a.m. the following Tuesday…that's three *harrowing* days and four *agonizing* nights, Your Honor…you were held captive by your own husband and in your own home. Do I have that correct?"

"That's correct." Sylvia risked a glance at Carl, seated mere yards from her in an ill-fitting suit. He fumed at Sylvia. Next to him, his lawyer looked nonplussed as he scribbled notes.

Joseph addressed the judge. "Your Honor, for nearly *one hundred hours*, Sylvia Owens was held hostage in her own home. Her crime? Attempting to prevent the murders of innocent people. People she didn't even know. Perfect strangers. In fact…"

Sylvia allowed the droning of Joseph Beech to fade into the background. The sounds of the courtroom washed over her without distinction.

When it was Carl's turn on the stand, he squirmed in the seat, slicking his hair back often and running a finger between his shirt collar and sweating neck.

As Sylvia had most dreaded, Carl's defense attorney led with the most damning evidence: Carl's testimony that Sylvia had had an affair with Jane King years prior. With Lonnie dead—mysteriously, as far as the court knew—the trail to finding out what happened to Jane went cold. Jane had not been seen by neighbors or friends. Her sisters had received letters over the years, but it now became clear that perhaps they hadn't been from Jane after all. It was to remain an open missing persons case for the time being. Perhaps Sylvia would get some answers eventually.

Even out of the hot seat, Sylvia was sweating with the announcement of her relationship with Jane. The most private moments of her life were now out in the open: not only that she'd had an affair, but that it was with a woman. What would people think of her? Sylvia did her best to avoid eye contact with anyone but Molly, who sat on one of the hard wooden chairs in the gallery.

Joseph questioned Carl in a clear, booming voice. "Mr. Owens, do you consider yourself a rational man?"

"I like to think so, yes."

"Not one to fly off the handle?"

"Well, perhaps at times. I can get...heated." Carl's smug look made Sylvia sick. The words he'd shout at her came echoing in her head. The snide remarks he'd made over so many years. The downright hatred he seemed to have for her throughout their marriage. *Heated, my ass.*

"And how long does such a feeling last?"

"Only a short while, depending on the issue, I'd say."

"Days? Weeks?"

Carl frowned, confused. "I suppose I calm down after a day or two."

"*A day or two.* I see...I see." Joseph thought for a moment. "Then why, sir, do you expect this court to believe that when you kidnapped your wife, drove her around for hours, and then locked her away in a room, that you were acting under duress—several *years* after you caught her *in flagrante delicto*? Mr. Owens, that's hardly the heat of the moment."

Carl was struck silent. Sylvia looked at Carl's lawyer, who only shrugged at Carl.

Joseph Beech presented into evidence the reels of recorded conversations that Molly and James had captured in Sylvia's home. He turned on the playback machine. The wheels clicked into place and the tape slowly pulled through the spools.

Through the speakers came Carl's voice. Sylvia cringed hearing it. "*Aw, don't give me that crap, King. I know you hired him. And sent those phony letters too! Like I wouldn't see through that after we faked the one for Sylvia. I told you that shit wouldn't work on her, dumb as she is. And it sure as hell didn't work on me. I hired you to kill those fags and goddamn it, you're going to do it!*"

"That's not fair!" Carl shouted, standing up from his seat next to the judge. "I was tricked. He's not a detective at all!" Carl scanned the faces in the courtroom, perhaps looking for whoever he was implicating. But James had not been subpoenaed. At the moment, he was recuperating in his hospital room. He'd given a sworn statement that had already been read by Joseph for the record.

The judge banged his gavel. "Please sit down, Mr. Owens. I will not have a spectacle."

Once Carl had resumed his seat, Joseph continued. "I assure you, Mr. Owens, James Hayward's occupation is not on trial here. What concerns this court today is what *you yourself* wrote in these lists and letters and speeches. What *you yourself* have said on these recordings. The actions that *you yourself* have taken, regardless of what heartache you may have suffered." Joseph addressed the elderly judge. "In any case, Your Honor, there *was* a private investigator present on the scene."

Joseph then switched on the recording again. The room listened intently. "*Molly Malone, private detective. You're in big trouble, Councilman. You too, Chief. I know all about the murders…*"

Sylvia and Molly locked eyes while the recording played. There was murmur among the crowd. Sylvia watched the startled and confused faces of the crowd gathered in the courtroom. People whispered and looked around the room, but only a few knew Molly Malone by sight.

Lonnie's voice rang out with a cackle over the speaker: "*A dyke detective! Imagine that!*"

The judge banged his gavel to quiet the gathering whispers of the courtroom. "Order, please."

Joseph turned off the recording.

"Objection." Carl's lawyer piped up.

Joseph laughed sharply. "For what?"

"Entrapment?"

"Your Honor, Ms. Malone is a legally operating *private*

detective. She was not presuming to act in the capacity of a political official or as a city police detective. Miss Malone was invited to the home that night by Mrs. Owens. And furthermore, Mr. Owens *asked* to be recorded during these events and then chose to confess his crimes. In what possible way is this entrapment?"

"Overruled." The judge looked weary. "Are we almost done, counselor?"

"Almost done, Your Honor. What's on trial here is not a governmental judgement about the social lives of homo-sexuals, but rather the revenge-based, cold-blooded murders of innocent people. I have a final piece of evidence, Your Honor. One that changes the direction of this entire trial."

"Out with it, then, Counselor," said the judge.

Joseph produced a stack of papers that made Sylvia's breath catch. She stole a look at Carl, whose stricken face told her what she knew would come. It was the speech Carl had been working on for so long, now presented as evidence in court.

"Do you recognize what this is, Mr. Owens?"

"Where did—how—this is…"

"Answer the question, please, Mr. Owens," intoned the judge.

"That is my private personal property—"

"The court will take that as a yes," Joseph said. "Your Honor, Exhibit F shows Mr. Owens's anticipation of the assassination of our very own Mayor Martin Booker. Further, this speech indicates that Mr. Owens expected to take Mayor Booker's place in the position."

Joseph stretched out a long arm to point dramatically at Carl. The tempo of his booming speech rolled along like that of a well-rehearsed preacher. "The man sitting here is not *only* responsible for ordering the murders of three private citizens and business owners. Mr. Owens admits this was his plan and motive all along. But let's not forget, Your Honor, that Carl Owens *also* instigated a plan of political bribery, police corruption, and graft—in total disregard for Mayor Booker's leadership. His end goal to be the mayor of the very city whose reputation he has tarnished would be laughable if it were not so alarming.

"Your Honor, ladies and gentlemen of the jury, that Carl Owens is guilty of these crimes is obvious. In considering the consequence of such actions, you must consider that this is a man who, when in fear of being found out for his misdeeds, made a choice so lowly, so cowardly, so *weak* as to use physical force and violence to kidnap his own wife. To hold someone hostage rather than take responsibility for his *own* actions. This adds the charge of *kidnapping* to Mr. Owens's lengthy list of crimes. The evidence I've presented today exposes a corrupt politician who hired San Francisco's chief of police to act as his own personal hitman. For these crimes, Your Honor, I ask you to consider the maximum sentence for Carl Owens. Life without parole. The prosecution rests."

When the jury read the verdict, Sylvia barely heard anything. But the beaming smiles on the faces of Joseph, Thomas, and Molly told her what she needed to know: they'd won.

Following the trial, Sylvia was awarded an expedited

divorce by the City of San Francisco, given the nature of Carl's monstrous crimes. She was also rewarded with most of his vast fortune, less Joseph Beech's fat cut. Sizable though the lawyer's fees were, Sylvia would be able to live with a comfortable financial cushion, and finally out from under Carl's thumb.

CHAPTER
TWENTY

James sat upright in the hospital bed, the newspaper splayed across his lap. Seated at his side, Lewis called to their visitor at the door: "It's open!"

The door to James's hospital room squeaked as Molly shuffled in.

"Speak of the devil," James said. Lewis stood from his chair next to James's bed and gave Molly a kind but tired smile. He then excused himself from the room, giving Molly's shoulder a squeeze on the way out.

"One bottle? What happened to a case?" James inspected the label on the champagne bottle Molly had set on the rickety hospital table next to him.

She immediately burst into tears. "I'm so sorry you got hurt! It's all my fault. I didn't listen. I knew you were done long ago and I just kept *pushing* you. I'm so sorry, James. I don't expect you to forgive me, but I—"

"Molly. It's alright. We're okay. I promise." James

reached for Molly's hand and gripped it. "I've had enough days lying in this bed to make peace with what happened. You're right that you didn't listen to me for months and you kept pushing me. But also...I kept coming back." James shrugged. "I could have quit anytime, but I didn't. But none of that matters anymore. It's over now. We both know that I'm done." James smiled softly at Molly and pointed to the thick cast on her arm. "It might help that you're busted up, too."

Molly laughed. "You can't quit, I'm firing you," she joked, wiping away her tears.

James looked askance at Molly. "You're pushing it, Malone."

"Alright. The truth is, I'm closing up shop anyway. Moving back home to Portland."

"Portland? What will you do there?"

"Start an agency again. But I'll do it right this time. No secrets."

"None?"

She smiled. "Maybe just the one. Sylvia's coming with me. We both need to get out of this town. In any case, Mayor Booker made it clear that as much as he appreciates the work we did to uncover the corruption under his nose, he'd prefer if I do my investigating...*elsewhere*. He all but begged me to find another beat. You may have heard that the city agreed to a settlement for the families of the victims—your friend Gene, as well as the owners of the Hot Spot and Duke's. Needless to say, our investigation cost the city quite a few clams. Which prompted Booker to kindly ask me to skedaddle. So, Portland it is."

"Back from whence you came." James considered this, then shrugged. "I'll miss you, boss."

And with that, fresh tears streamed down Molly's cheeks. With her good arm, she did her best to hug James again.

Lewis entered the room quietly, allowing space for James and Molly to complete their moment.

Molly gestured him over and indicated the bottle of champagne. "Do the honors, Lew?"

"Certainly!" Lewis collected three paper cups from next to the small tin sink in the hospital room and popped the cork on the bottle.

"I brought you something else," Molly said to James.

"Dare I ask?"

From her briefcase, Molly pulled out a collection of small pieces of electronic miscellany, all wires and switches. "Red light, green light," Molly said as she laid out the disassembled alert system from above the detective office door. "And here are the switches from inside the drawer."

James could only laugh at the collection of broken knobs and gadgets. "I'll drink to that, Detective Malone."

CHAPTER
TWENTY-ONE

Several weeks later, Molly sat in the dim red glow of Whiskers. The jukebox sang a bright and easy song. Around the tables, people danced closely to the softly sensuous rhythm. Molly's cast had been recently removed and her arm was nicely healed, though the scarring was still bright and unbearable to look at.

Sylvia was snuggled close beside Molly, their fingers entwined. They'd moved past accidental close kisses in Molly's car to spending every waking moment together, not to mention nights too. What they'd gone through together was horrid. Now on the other side of it, they'd fallen easily into a relationship in a matter of weeks.

Without hesitation, Molly knew she was ready again. She knew she'd be different with Sylvia. She already was. Sylvia had opened her heart in ways she'd always known she needed. From the moment Sylvia had held the lingering gaze in her office, Molly had known there was something about her she'd been waiting for.

On the other side of Sylvia sat James, looking much more alive than the last time she'd seen him. He nodded at Molly from across the table, one hand on Lewis's thigh. Next to James, Lewis regaled the group with a slightly embellished story of James's experience in the hospital. "—after that, she wasn't *just* my favorite nurse anymore, she also earned a spot at our monthly bridge parties."

Next to Lewis sat Thomas Parker, thrilled with Lewis's storytelling. Joseph Beech sat close to Thomas, one arm around the back of his chair.

Joseph offered a toast. "To Detective Parker, who just today was promoted to head of vice squad, in light of recent events."

Thomas and Molly shared uneasy smiles that the rest of the group seemed to miss. Sidling up behind Molly, Paula gently set down a full bottle of whiskey in the center of the group's table.

"By orders of Uncle Val."

When Molly read that Lonnie King's death was ruled an accident and even the newspapers downplayed his death as simply a risk of the job, she understood just how far Valentino Fazio's influence reached. Which is why she was relieved to be getting out of San Francisco and heading back north to Portland. Mayor Booker's one-way ticket was generous, if not slightly alarming in his insistence that she take it. Regardless, she relished the idea of starting a new life together with Sylvia. A fresh start for both of them.

As Paula turned to leave, Molly excused herself from the table. She pulled Paula aside and spoke in a hushed tone. "I appreciate all the nice things he's doing. I really do. But it's not necessary anymore. I'm just glad you're alright. Can't we let it go? Call it even?"

Paula sighed. With a glance to the back hallway, she shook her head slightly. "Uncle Val doesn't work that way, I'm afraid."

"What does that mean?"

"It means *he* decides when you're even." Paula dried her hands on a bar towel she'd tossed over one shoulder. "But listen, let me know when you get settled in Portland. I'll make sure to visit you and Sylvia when I'm up that way. Don't be surprised if you see Natalia up there too. And stop by before you leave—I'll send you with some bottles." Paula gave Molly a good-natured slap on the back.

In her head, Molly heard what Valentino had said only days before killing Lonnie: *I do not* have *connections. I am the connection.* Thankfully, Valentino's operations were strongly concentrated in the Bay. Molly would feel much better when she and Sylvia had set up their new life far away from it all.

When Molly returned to the table, Joseph had opened the fresh bottle of whiskey and was pouring more for the group.

Sylvia whispered into Molly's ear, "Cheers, darling. To the rest of our days." Molly kissed her then, as well as she could through the goofy grins that played across their mouths.

The final high notes of the song on the jukebox

sounded clearly through the candlelit evening. The lyrics echoed the swelling sentiment in Molly's heart:

> *You are the breathless hush of evening that trembles on the brink of a lovely song…*

"To the vice mongers," Lewis offered, and they all drank.

AUTHOR'S NOTES

The Atherton Report came out of an investigation conducted by private detective Edwin Atherton in 1935 (released as a report in 1937). Though Atherton was not hired specifically by the mayor, as he was in this book, his detailed report revealed immense corruption throughout the San Francisco Police Force.

My fictional Mayor Martin Booker says, "We learned through the experience of prohibition that people's morals and habits cannot be changed by legislation." In truth, it was Edwin Atherton who said those words in his 1937 report. Atherton was, perhaps surprisingly, an advocate for legalizing many of the places and activities that had been deemed illegal. Atherton went on to say:

"Statutes which conflict with the laws of human nature are unenforceable and the open flouting of such laws by a large percentage of the people creates disrespect for the law in general.

Those persons, who think that prostitution and gambling are stopped because of prohibitive legislation, must be likened to the ostrich of popular repute."

In *Dear Sylvia, Love Jane*, fictional police chief Lonnie King says, "I had trouble telling which were the men and which were the women." Those words actually came from San Francisco Police Sergeant Glen Hughes, as he reflected on a police raid of Mona's Tavern in 1938.

Ohlone Street, where Molly's office is located, doesn't exist in San Francisco as far as my research has found. I named the street for the Muwekma Ohlone Tribe on whose ancestral and unceded land this story is set.

REFERENCES

Atherton, Edwin. *Report to the 1937 Grand Jury on Graft in the San Francisco Police Department*. Submitted by Atherton and Dunn Investigations, March 17, 1937. Released by Superior Court Judge Franklin A. Griffin, April 1939.

Boyd, Nan Alamilla. *Wide Open Town: A History of Queer San Francisco to 1965*. University of California Press, 2003.

Bronski, Michael. *A Queer History of the United States*, Beacon Press, 2011.

Crawford Jr., Phillip. *The Mafia and the Gays*. 2015.

—. *Queer Joints, Wiseguys and G-Men*. 2019.

Kaiser, Charles. *The Gay Metropolis: The Landmark History of Gay Life in America*. Grove Press, 2019.

ACKNOWLEDGMENTS

First and foremost and forever: to Amanda—thank you for vegan nachos, coffee with oat milk, CBD sodas, for trips to the beach when I'm stuck on a chapter, and for your thoughtful questions and feedback on plot, character motivation, and motive. Thank you for believing in me the whole way through, even when I wanted to quit. Thank you for so much more than I can capture here.

Huge thank-yous to my editing team at Indigo: Editing, Design, and More—Melissa Ousley, Bailey Potter, Sarah Currin. Thank you for flagging errors, pointing out inconsistencies, offering alternative options for tricky scenes, and for providing insights that helped shape this book into a much more palatable morsel. Any errors or confusing bits are mine alone. Find these fine folks at indgoediting.com. To Indigo's fearless leader Ali Shaw: it's been a joy to orbit your professional world since those long-ago Ooligan days. Thank you for helping me get my book out into the world.

Lesbihonest, if you didn't like my book, you have to admit it's beautiful. From the first conversation I had with Jenifer Prince, I knew she'd be a dream to work with. Jenifer, you captured Molly and Sylvia's images perfectly, and were able to turn my sketchy concept into a beautiful cover that has resonated with so many people. I am eternally grateful to you for this collaboration and I greatly look forward to future ones.

Thanks also to Elizabeth Mitchell and Kate Ristau for coffee chats, co-writing time, answering my unending questions about writing and publishing, and generally for just being rad people. You've both inspired me more than you know, not only because of your hair.

To my beta readers, Jackson Warner and Amanda Hagen: your notes, insights, questions, and suggestions were invaluable. Thank you for your heartfelt close readings, your encouragement, and your wisdom. (Ready for book two?)

ABOUT THE AUTHOR

Erin Hall (she/her) is a writer, small business marketing coach, writing instructor, book reviewer, and bookseller. She lives and writes in Oregon's Willamette Valley. This is her first book. Find her at ehallwrites.com.

www.ingramcontent.com/pod-product-compliance
Lightning Source LLC
Chambersburg PA
CBHW021353150726
47989CB00005B/2231